BLOOD
TIES

BLOOD TIES

JENNY FRANCIS

Copyright © 2016 Jenny Francis

The moral right of the author has been asserted.

Apart from any fair dealing for the purposes of research or private study, or criticism or review, as permitted under the Copyright, Designs and Patents Act 1988, this publication may only be reproduced, stored or transmitted, in any form or by any means, with the prior permission in writing of the publishers, or in the case of reprographic reproduction in accordance with the terms of licences issued by the Copyright Licensing Agency. Enquiries concerning reproduction outside those terms should be sent to the publishers.

This is a work of fiction. Names, characters, businesses, places, events and incidents are either the products of the author's imagination or used in a fictitious manner. Any resemblance to actual persons, living or dead, or actual events is purely coincidental.

Matador
9 Priory Business Park,
Wistow Road, Kibworth Beauchamp,
Leicestershire. LE8 0RX
Tel: 0116 279 2299
Email: books@troubador.co.uk
Web: www.troubador.co.uk/matador
Twitter: @matadorbooks

ISBN 978 1785893 797

British Library Cataloguing in Publication Data.
A catalogue record for this book is available from the British Library.

Printed and bound in the UK by TJ International, Padstow, Cornwall
Typeset in 11pt Aldine401 BT by Troubador Publishing Ltd, Leicester, UK

Matador is an imprint of Troubador Publishing Ltd

Dedicated to the fight to stop the bullies.

AUTHOR'S NOTE

Blood Ties is the second Detective Inspector Charlie Moon novel. Like the first, The Silent Passage, it is set in Birmingham at the time of the millennium. Team Penda is a fictional creation and the story of how it came into being following the disbanding of the West Midlands Serious Crimes Squad in 1989 is told in an appendix at the end of the book.

Moon is back on the scene two years on from his suspension from duty for breaking house rules but the feeling is still there his superiors are out to get him.

Jenny Francis
2016

Visit www.meetjennyfrancis.com to find out more about books by Jenny Francis.

PRELUDE

Waiting for Mum and Dad to come back

It was always the same when Mum and Dad went out. They were gone for hours and she was left on her own watching the clock go round waiting for them to come back. This time it was shopping or so Mum said as she buttoned up her coat. Just popping to Tesco's and perhaps we'll stop off and have a cup of tea with Aunty Lil and Uncle Ted on the way home. Shan't be long, that was at ten to three. Shan't be long, now it was half past five and getting dark outside.

She went over to the front window and saw the streetlights were coming on and a coal tit performing somersaults on the bird feeder in next door's garden. She watched it for a while. She wondered what Mum and Dad would say when they walked through the door. Sorry, luvvie, we've been gone longer than we thought. Still not to worry, eh, we'll soon have some tea on the table once we've got the shopping put away. Not cross with us, are you? Not going to spend the rest of the night with a sulky look on your face?

A woman with a child in a pushchair went by then, on the other side of the street, a boy carrying a football. She turned to Tilly. Tilly was sitting on the sofa where she always sat with her legs splayed out and her back up against a cushion. Tilly needed a new frock. One of Tilly's arms needed stitching back on but, as usual, Tilly said nothing.

What Mum and Dad didn't know though were the thoughts that went through her head when she was on her own, thoughts she shared with no one not even Tilly. Mum and Dad growing old. Mum and Dad not there anymore and home, a room in a place that smelled like a hospital.

Tilly was asleep now, curled up on the cushion. She went back to looking out of the window. Waiting for Mum and Dad to come back and hoping they wouldn't be long.

CHAPTER ONE

The Body in the Woods

FEBRUARY 2001

It had been a good start to the day for Detective Inspector Charlie Moon. First came the news that his boss Willoughby had gone down with laryngitis forcing him to take to his sick bed and robbing him temporarily of his power of speech. It meant there'd be no Willoughby on the phone every minute of the day and night and Moon would have chance to get on with the job without the Team Penda Commander breathing down his neck all the time.

Then, best of all, the discovery back at base that the IT systems had gone down. No email and Willoughby's one remaining line of communication taken away; the irony being the internet and email system had been Willoughby's pet project from the beginning.

And, just when he thought things couldn't get any better, the phone call earlier on to say a body had been discovered in woodland on the rural fringes of the West Midlands offering the rare chance of a pleasant drive out into the country. All in the line of duty, of course.

It wasn't long before he left the sprawl of the towns

behind. In front the road stretched ahead crossing hill and dale with hedgerows on either side either neatly trimmed or wild and ragged with festoons of travellers' joy and trailers of bright red bryony berries. Redwings and mistle thrushes flew up and overhead a pale watery sun did its best to peep through the clouds. He slipped on a CD of scratchy Tommy Johnson recordings from the late 1920s – one he hadn't listened to for a while – and let his thoughts drift off to nowhere in particular. Few cars on the road. No one bothering him. Time to sit back and enjoy the simple things in life.

A turn to the right, he almost missed it, then along a narrow twisting lane for half a mile until he came to the place where police cars and vans were pulled over on the verge. A uniformed constable stepped out to check his ID then directed him to a field gateway where there was just enough room to park. Moon noticed at once the crime scene tapes sectioning off an area of trees bordering the left hand side of the lane. He checked his watch. Ten past two. He got out of the car and retrieved his overcoat from the back seat. A familiar figure was coming towards him: Detective Sergeant Dave Thompson sticking out like a sore thumb in his bright yellow all weather coat that had gone a bit grubby at the cuffs and needed a visit to the dry cleaners.

'You'll need a pair of these,' said Thompson pointing to the wellingtons on his feet.

Moon nodded and went round to the boot of the car where he kept a whole range of items he might need when called on as now to inspect a crime scene in the middle of nowhere. As soon as he'd changed out of his shoes he rejoined Thompson standing in the middle of the lane taking in all the activity going on in front of them. The body had been found two days earlier by a man walking his dog. The decision to bring in serious crimes officers from Team Penda had been taken twenty four hours later when it was discovered the body belonged to someone who came from outside the area and had connections in the criminal world.

'Local CID felt it was out of their league,' Thompson explained. Thompson had been despatched to the scene at the crack of dawn with a brief to find out what was going on.

'Is this someone passing the buck?' said Moon who'd been caught out before by detectives taking the easy way out with cases that called for more than the standard level of effort.

'Could be,' Thompson shrugged but any further discussion of the subject was curtailed by the approach of one of the Crime Scene Officers who had detached himself from the group standing in a huddle further down the lane.

'We've finished what we need to do,' he said after an exchange of introductions then explained that he and his colleagues had been over the area of trees and adjoining land with a fine toothcomb. 'All we've come across is a rusty horseshoe, a dead owl and three used condoms looking like they'd been there since before Christmas.'

'Do we have any more on the cause of death?' Moon directed his question at both of them. Thompson answered. 'They carried out a preliminary examination of the cadaver before they bagged it up. Gunshot wounds to the head and chest. A shotgun fired at close range.' The Crime Scene Officer nodded. 'Not a pretty sight. Not what I'd want to be looking at before breakfast.'

'What about spent cartridges?' Moon asked making a mental note to have another word with Thompson about referring to dead bodies as cadavers.

The Crime Scene Officer shook his head. 'Whoever did it must have taken them away. Our people have been up and down the lane and searched the ditches and hedgerows on both sides just in case someone threw them out of a car window.'

'Or maybe the shooting took place somewhere else and the body was just dumped here.'

Again the officer shook his head. 'We've found bits of bone and brains splattered all over the place. Not to mention the pieces of shot we've dug out of the trunks of the trees. No, here was where it happened all right. No doubts on that score.'

The Crime Scene Officer drifted off to rejoin the rest of his party who were busy packing up to go. Moon and Thompson meanwhile pushed their way through a gap in the hedge that separated the trees from the lane. There was a path of sorts passing between a dense undergrowth of ferns and brambles flattened down here and there by the Crime Scene Officers going about their work. The trees, Moon noticed, were a mix of ancient oak and silver birch. About fifty yards into the woodland they came to a small clearing.

'This is where the body was found' said Thompson pointing to an area of ground thick in leaf mould and showing signs of scuff marks made by the comings and goings of officers' heavy boots.

'What do we know about him so far?' Moon said casting his eyes around.

'A man in his late twenties named Sean Mattox. They identified him pretty quickly from his fingerprints.'

'Not a local?'

'No, from Hereford,' Thompson replied. 'At least that was his last known address.'

'What's his form?'

'Apart from regularly being caught driving without tax and insurance, most of the trouble he's been in stems from handling stolen goods. Short terms in prison, the most recent being eighteen months ago.'

'Have you checked this out?'

Thompson nodded. 'I spoke to a Sergeant Kite in Hereford who has felt his collar a few times. It seems he operated as a go-between. You want a new telly or a hi-fi and the word on the street was ask Sean. Fancied himself as a bit of a wheeler-dealer.'

'Drugs?'

'Found once with some cannabis in his pockets. Nothing to suggest he was supplying the stuff.'

Thompson brought out a small camera from his coat pocket and started taking photographs. Moon meanwhile carried on looking round trying to get a mental picture of what had taken place here. When Thompson finished they carried on walking following the footpath as it wound through the trees until they came to a fence line separating the woods from a ploughed field that stretched off into the distance. Here they stopped, Moon noticing the sun getting lower in the sky and a reminder it was still winter.

'Any thoughts Dave?'

Thompson looked at him. 'Your guess is as good as mine. What do people get up to in the middle of a wood? Poaching? Looking for mushrooms? Dogging perhaps?'

'Doggers don't usually go round armed with shotguns.'

'No Guv.'

'And they say nothing ever happens in the country,' said Moon turning away and transferring his attention to a flock of wood pigeons picking around among the ridges and furrows halfway across the field.

Back at Moon's car they noticed the police presence in the lane had thinned down. Just a handful of uniformed officers standing around ready to see off any members of the public who took it into their heads to come and check out what was going on before it got dark.

★★★

It was on the dot of ten next morning when Moon put his head round the door of Doctor Lionel Moet's office.

'Charlie,' said Moet getting up to shake his hand. Moet, better known as Nell to his associates, had been the A to Z of forensic pathology in the West Midlands for more years than anybody could remember. 'You old dog, how's life treating you these days?'

'Could be better, could be worse,' said Moon casting his eyes around the untidy piles of paper and general disarray in which Nell chose to work. Rumour had it the eminent pathologist, who shared names with a leading brand of champagne, had been told to cut down on his alcohol intake but no one was sure whether this was on medical advice or an instruction from higher authority. Certainly there was no sign of the bottle of single malt that usually came out when senior police officers came calling. Instead Nell led Moon through to a small kitchen where a coffee machine was bubbling in the corner.

'How do you take this stuff?' said Nell pouring coffee into a plastic cup.

'Black, no sugar' Moon replied.

Moon then followed Nell along a corridor steeling himself for what was coming next. Time to take a look at the victim or what remained of him and the part of the job Moon with his ticklish stomach looked forward to least.

'Down at the end,' said Nell as they passed through a set of double doors into a large open area where two members of his team were working. Moon's normal tactic at this point was to avert his eyes from what was going on, concentrating instead on not spilling his coffee.

'Here's your boy,' said Nell flicking on a set of high-powered lamps over the furthest in a row of post-mortem examination tables where the body of a slightly-built man of medium height lay.

Moon blinked. Although he had a good idea what to expect, most victims of shootings that came his way were gangland killings where the murder weapon was nothing bigger than a handgun. In contrast Mattox had a massive chest wound through which all sorts of viscera were poking out. Even worse was the man's head of which little remained apart from the back of his skull. The whole of his face had been shot away.

'You're dripping coffee down your sleeve,' said Nell looking across at him.

'Not all the damage you see was done by the shooting,' Nell explained after a pause to adjust his half-moon spectacles so he could examine the man's naked torso more closely. 'There is evidence animals have been at work here, here and here.'

'Animals?'

'Foxes, rodents and corvids such as rooks and magpies: they've all had a nibble at him at some point. Consistent with our friend's body being exposed out in the open for a few days.'

'Time of death?'

Nell pursed his lips. 'I'd say middle to end of last week judging from the general state of the body. We might be able to get a more accurate idea when we've done the full PM.'

'Anything else we need to know before we start investigating?'

Nell smiled. 'I'm not sure if it's relevant but take a look at this.' He was pointing to the man's genitals. 'He's got a dose of the clap. Good old-fashioned gonorrhoea by the looks of it. Still, that's the least of his worries now.'

The queasy feeling in Moon's insides started to wear off as soon as they got back into Nell's office.

'Am I getting the right picture here?' Moon began when they were both seated. 'Someone shot him once in the chest and then again in the face. We don't know why but one theory could be someone wanted to make sure he was dead.'

Nell put his feet up on the desk. 'You could be right Charlie. Ballistics think the shot to the head was fired at a closer range and from a different angle consistent with our friend going down with the chest wound then someone having another pot at him when he was on the ground just to finish him off.'

'The chest wound would have been fatal?'

'Without a doubt but, as you suggest, perhaps someone wanted to be certain he didn't live to tell the tale. Or another thought I had was an amateurish attempt to make it harder to identify him. No face and no teeth, if you see what I mean.'

'A double-barrelled shotgun?'

'A reasonably safe assumption. Bang, one trigger, then two steps forward and bang again. Has anybody told you about the way he was dressed?'

'Not so far.'

'Light cotton short-sleeved shirt, chinos and a fancy pair of trainers. Not what you'd expect someone to be wearing out of doors in the middle of winter. All a bit odd if you ask me.'

***

Moon's drive back to the office took him through busy inner city backstreets lined with cars parked along both sides. As was his usual habit, he kept his eyes on the rear-view mirror checking who was behind and never putting it past Willoughby and his pals to have someone tailing him in the way they'd done before. In truth the last two years had witnessed an uneasy truce between Moon and the top brass of Team Penda. The feeling his every move was being watched had never gone away. Moon, for his part, had done his best to keep his head down, putting on a big show of going along with everything, yet knowing in his heart of hearts Willoughby was no fool.

However, the first sight that greeted Moon when he arrived at HQ brought a smile to his lips. Boffins from IT walking round with frowns on their faces signalling to him the problems with the server still hadn't been fixed. He made his way through to the small conference room where Thompson was already in the process of bringing Detective Constables Scott and Tamberlin up to speed. Taped to the whiteboard on the wall, along with a selection of photographs from the crime scene, was a 1:25000 series Ordnance Survey map of the area which Thompson had acquired from somewhere.

Scott was speaking as Moon walked in and pulled up a chair. 'It would help if we knew what Mattox was doing up in this part of the world. If he had connections locally someone must know something.'

Thompson grinned. 'Thanks Scotty. I'll put you down for going round knocking on doors. I know how much you like the fresh air.'

Before Scott had chance to reply Moon butted in and gave them a quick run-down on his visit to the mortuary.

'This geezer's not had a lot of luck,' Tamberlin commented. 'First someone gives him the pox then he ends up having most of his head shot off. It doesn't get much worse when you think about it.'

'Try working here,' Scott muttered gloomily.

Moon turned to Thompson. 'Any more from Hereford Dave?'

'Not a lot Guv. Sergeant Kite reckons Mattox hasn't been seen down there since before Christmas. The flat where he lived has been repossessed. The landlord is furious because a load of the fixtures and fittings have gone missing.'

'Like what?'

'Bathroom taps, door knobs, even two of the radiators have been taken off the walls.'

'What about family, known associates?'

'Sergeant Kite thinks there's a brother living in Cardiff but, as far as he knows, they haven't spoken to one another for years. The people he knocked round with in Hereford know nothing or they say they know nothing although a few of them mentioned he was shacked up with a woman but they don't know where.'

'Sarge.' It was Tamberlin who spoke. 'Shouldn't we be investigating the poaching angle? It seems the most likely explanation for what he was doing wandering round in a wood.'

Thompson nodded. 'I put that suggestion to Sergeant Kite. Was Mattox into fixing people up with a brace of pheasants? His reply was he wouldn't put it past Mattox to be involved in anything that would earn him a few quid. His form though was for the kind of stuff that comes off the back of trucks: electrical goods, bottles of spirits, cigarettes, that kind of thing.'

'Well,' said Moon. 'Unless anyone's got anything else to say I suggest we start by getting together a list of licensed shotgun owners. We can start off with a five mile radius of the crime scene and work outwards if we have to. Dave, can I leave that with you? Tambo you team up with Scotty and see what you can find out from talking to the locals. Gossip, anything that will give us some clues about what goes on up these quiet country lanes that would interest the likes of Mattox. Talk to the postman, the bin men, the nosy parkers. See if they've seen anything unusual going on and, if necessary, jog their memories.'

Doing a detour to check his emails and finding to his relief that his inbox was still empty Moon decided to make his next port of call the sandwich shop two blocks away where he'd been a regular customer since the day it opened six months ago. On his way out he spotted DI Millership driving in through the gates. Next to Willoughby, Millership topped the list of the people Moon least wished to see. According to the jokers on the team Millership was in line for the Police Medal for brown-nosing and an invitation to Buckingham Palace in the not too distant future. Millership, however, had earned his place next to the throne in Team Penda by acting as Willoughby's eyes and ears not just licking his boots. Charlie Moon was in no doubt Millership had seen him nipping off and would be noting it down so he could feed it back to Willoughby the next time he saw him.

After purchasing a ham salad baguette from the sandwich shop he drove the half mile or so to a piece of derelict land overlooking one of the railway lines into the city. Here he relived boyhood memories of watching trains go by although he no longer wrote down their numbers. When he'd finished the baguette he reached over to the glove compartment where he kept a packet of wet wipes. There his eyes fell on a box set of CDs he'd bought for two pounds in a charity shop just before Christmas. The early recordings of Lowell Fulson, intended as a present for someone he'd not seen for a long time but someone he'd be seeing again sooner than he thought.

Woodland

Ridge

spinney

↑ N

Cottage

Four Lanes End

To the village

|———————| One Mile

CHAPTER TWO

Four Lanes End

A FEW WEEKS EARLIER

Tim's first day at the cottage started with a shopping trip. A development had sprung up on the edge of the nearby town with a supermarket, DIY store, garden centre and a place selling camping and caravan accessories. Now he had everything he needed and enough food to keep him going for the rest of the week. Free to turn his thoughts to what he'd been looking forward to most: getting out and exploring his new surroundings; discovering where all the little lanes and by-ways went.

The cottage ticked all the boxes from the day he first saw it. Off the beaten track and two miles from the nearest village, it offered sanctuary, somewhere to make a new start and space to think.

He set off with two hours of daylight left and, while the wind from the north-west was fresh, the sun felt pleasant on his face. It was only a short walk up to the crossroads which gave the cottage its name: Four Lanes End, a place where he paused for a few moments to take in the view and pick out the village nestling in the dale below. He thought about which way to go and chose right, the opposite direction to the village, and up a lane which looked neglected and little used. Soon he found himself in a world enclosed by steep banks and overhanging hedgerows but he'd not been walking long before the lane opened up and he came to a gate on the left where he paused again. A flock of sheep grazing in a field on the other side and, beyond the field, another rising up towards a ridgeline. He took out the small pair of binoculars he'd thought to put in his coat pocket. Near to the crest of the ridge he picked out a fallen tree with a large bird sitting on the stump that could have been a buzzard. Over to the right what looked like an old piece of farm machinery left to go rusty in the corner of the field.

On he went, noticing the lane getting steeper, the strip of green grass growing down the middle and his new boots starting to rub. He saw no one. He heard nothing apart from the wind, the sheep over in the field and the sound of someone a long way off working a chainsaw.

He'd gone about a mile when he first had the feeling he was being followed. He stopped and turned, half-expecting to see another walker out enjoying the fresh air, but there was nobody there. Just the two ribbons of tarmac and the tall raggedy hedgerows stretching back as far as he could see but otherwise nothing apart from the scattering of fleecy clouds racing across the sky driven by the wind. He took out the binoculars again and held them to his eyes. A partridge picking its way along the verge moving in and out of cover until it finally disappeared. In the hedges, the bright reds and oranges of haws and hips caught in the sunlight while pale yellow hazel catkins quivered delicately in the breeze.

He put the binoculars back in his pocket telling himself the mind could play strange tricks in quiet and lonely places especially on those who, like him, had spent their lives living in towns.

He set off again, starting to feel the pull of the climb but at the same time determined to find where the lane went to even though he suspected it might come to a sudden end in a farmyard. He kept going then, coming over a rise, he caught sight of something up in front. On the right a spinney of trees but, just beyond it, what looked like the entrance to somewhere. A red shale driveway going off between two massive stone pillars flanked on either side by equally massive stone walls. A metal sign was attached to one of the pillars and, when he got close enough to read it, he saw it said:

PRIVATE ESTATE
KEEP OUT
NO PUBLIC RIGHT OF WAY
VISITORS BY APPOINTMENT ONLY

There was no gate but the entrance was protected by a cattle grid beyond which the driveway curved round a dense thicket of laurel bushes then disappeared. He carried on walking. The lane turned sharply to the left following the course of the wall but, after a short distance, it petered out into a muddy track.

He checked his watch. It was later than he thought and the sun was already starting to cast long shadows. Time to get back, he told himself, dreading to think how many blisters he'd find when he took his socks off. In front the track entered an area of scattered woodland while the wall went off at an angle where he lost sight of it disappearing into the trees. Private estate, keep out: he wondered what all the fuss was about and why someone had gone to such lengths to deter intruders. One way to find out was to take a look over the wall and here, in the cover of the trees, seemed like a good place to do it because nobody would see him.

A shallow ditch ran alongside the track which he stepped over after which he pushed his way through a few yards of underbrush until the wall stood in front of him. Ancient looking and built from blocks of rough-hewn local limestone, its height was difficult to judge but he found even at full stretch his fingertips scarcely managed to touch the coping stones at the top. Just then a voice spoke.

'I wouldn't do that if I was you.'

Tim turned round sharply. No more than ten feet away, stood a man with his back up against the trunk of a tree. On closer inspection he was an elderly man wearing a flat cap, an old-fashioned belted overcoat and carrying a stout looking stick in his hand. It was anyone's guess how long he'd been there.

'I'm sorry......' Tim stammered while at the same time racking his brains to think up a plausible excuse for what he was doing acting in a suspicious way in front of the wall to someone's private property.

'Don't apologise on my account,' said the man. 'I was just doing my best to offer you some advice. There's a bloody great brute of a dog roaming loose on the other side of that wall and, if you climbed over it, you could end up in hospital with pieces ripped out of your flesh. It's already happened to a few I could name. Poachers mostly.'

Tim studied the old man's face. It was lined like the bark of a tree but his eyes were bright and clear. Eyes that missed nothing.

'You're the gent who's moved into the cottage down by Four Lanes End,' the old man continued. 'I've seen you there a couple of times.'

'It's only temporary,' said Tim. 'I'm renting for a while until I can find something more permanent.'

'I wasn't prying into your business,' said the old man leaning forward on his stick. 'Just explaining how I come to know you. I pass your place often.'

'I'll keep an eye open for you.'

Just then a small fox terrier appeared out of the trees.

'Jack's been off on his own,' the old man smiled. 'He knows his way round these woods better than I do.'

'Do you live nearby?'

'If you call the village nearby.'

The fox terrier barked.

'He's telling me he wants to be off,' the old man explained. 'He doesn't like it when I stand talking. Still, I expect we'll meet again. Joe Darby's the name. What's yours?'

'Tim,' said Tim. 'Tim Stafford.'

The old man pointed with his stick to where a path went off into the trees. 'I'm going this way,' he said then, as he went to walk off, he turned round and called. 'Don't forget what I told you about keeping this side of that wall.'

'I won't,' Tim replied.

After he lost sight of the old man Tim retraced his steps back to the lane anxious to get going on the return leg of his walk before his sore feet started to feel any worse.

The light was starting to go as he went past the two giant pillars standing like sentinels on either side of the cattle grid. A roosting pheasant called out from the spinney and he quickened his pace, letting his thoughts turn to the log fire he'd light as soon as he got in and the joint of beef and bottle of Rhone he'd got planned for later.

It was hard to say when the feeling of being followed came back. At first he tried to ignore it but then he found he couldn't. He looked over his shoulder once, twice, he lost count of the number of times but, like before, there was never anybody there. Just the lane with its hedgerows and its strip of grass growing down the middle. He felt a nip in the air and, as the sun sank behind a line of distant hills, the first few stars started to come out.

He was hobbling by the time he got back to the crossroads where he paused, as he had done earlier, to take in the view. The village down in the dale where the streetlights were starting to come on and a thin trail of mist marked the course of the stream. The cottage was only a few steps away, nestling in a dip, and he could see the chimney pots clearly as he lingered a little longer soaking in the tranquillity while the world around him sank into shadows. Sounds in the distance; sheep settling down for the night, traffic on the main road but then something closer. He turned round sharply. Behind him the lane he'd just come down where all the shapes merged into one in the gathering gloom. He watched and listened. The seconds passed. An owl hooted from somewhere answered by another further off. His thoughts returned to getting his boots off and putting his feet in a bowl of hot water for a good long soak.

CHAPTER THREE

Too Early To Call

A FEW WEEKS LATER

Charlie Moon was in the doghouse. Not for the first time in his married life he'd forgotten it was parents' evening at the girls' school so Cathy had been left having to make apologies for his non-appearance by using the old excuse that his important job in the police force often called on him to work long and unsocial hours.

The atmosphere at breakfast time was still glacial and, as Moon drove off into the rush hour traffic, he made a mental note to add stopping off at the florists on the list of things to do today. Arriving at HQ he did his usual visual check of the cars parked outside. There were a few new ones he noticed, evidence the IT presence on site had been beefed up to deal with the gremlin in the system that had so far defied all attempts to winkle it out.

'Morning,' said Moon as he breezed past the familiar figure of Sergeant Hobbs on desk duty.

Thompson was already in the conference room. Scott and Tamberlin walked in soon after Moon.

The two young DCs had spent the afternoon before making door-to-door enquiries in the area immediately around the crime scene. In Scott's case the high point came when he was chased around a farmyard by a goat.

'It wasn't funny,' said Scott with a hurt expression on his face.

Tamberlin took up the story. 'It turned out some of the properties we called at are second homes – people from the city who've snapped up run-down cottages on the cheap then spent their spare cash on doing them up. In a lot of cases the owners are only there at weekends. The few we managed to track down couldn't tell us much.'

'What about everyone else?' said Thompson.

Scott answered. 'As we thought the betting locally is that this has something to do with poaching. Apparently there are rumours doing the rounds of organised gangs coming into the area and helping themselves to pheasants, even cows and sheep.'

'What about Mattox?' said Moon looking up. 'Have you spoken to anyone who knows him?'

Scott and Tamberlin both shook their heads. 'It's the sort of place where everyone knows everyone else,' Tamberlin explained. 'When we mentioned Mattox's name they all looked blank. No one has ever heard of him.'

'Is anyone hiding anything?'

'Sorry Guv.'

'I was just posing the question. Someone was responsible for shooting Mattox and whoever did it won't be falling over themselves admitting they know him. See what I'm driving at? Don't believe everything you're being told.'

'No Guv.'

Scott chipped in. 'Perhaps what we're looking at is Mattox being driven to where he was shot randomly. Someone wanted him dead so they bundled him in a car and drove up the first country lane they came to. We've not found a local connection because there isn't one.'

'It's a theory,' Moon admitted. 'But if someone planned all this wouldn't they have given a bit more thought to disposing of the body? Just leaving it under a pile of leaves for anybody to find doesn't strike me as the work of a clever criminal mind.'

Moon turned to Thompson. 'Dave what have we got so far on licensed shotgun owners?'

Thompson pushed across a sheet of paper. 'There's a list of them there. Mostly farmers and landowners so I'm told.'

Moon ran his eyes over the list.

'Have any of these got form?'

'No Guv.'

'What about links with the criminal fraternity?'

'I'm still asking round but so far nothing's come to light. Pillars of respectability in most cases, two of the names you're looking at are local magistrates.'

'Anything else Dave?'

'Just this.' He held up several sheets of paper that had been stapled together at the corner. 'It was faxed over first thing this morning by Forensics. It's the results of their tests on Mattox's clothes.'

'What's it say? Stick to the interesting bits. It's too early in the morning for science lessons.'

'Fibres on his shirt and trousers, the sort of fibres that could have come off a car seat. A human hair that wasn't his. Two pounds or thereabouts in loose change in his pockets. Some of the mud on the soles of his trainers matches the mud from where he was found but some of it doesn't.'

'Go on.'

'They've found traces of pine needles or, to be exact, needles from larch trees. Samples of soil from the crime scene show no evidence of any sort of pine needles so they must have come from somewhere else.'

'Is that it?'

'Not quite. They think he paddled across a stream or a pond at some point. There's evidence of water marks on his trousers. Up to and over his knees apparently.'

'Sounds to me like someone doing a runner,' said Scott.

Moon looked at him. 'You may be right Scotty but let's not jump to conclusions too hastily. Dave…'

'Yes Guv.'

'Before this case was dumped on us did anybody bother to find out who owns the land where Mattox was found. Is it private property or can anybody go and have a wander round?'

Thompson went over to the OS map that was still taped to the whiteboard. 'It's called Wrox Wood,' he said pointing to the area circled with red marker pen. 'According to what I've found out so far it's had a chequered history. It used to be part of a big estate then a property developer bought it in the early nineties with the idea of felling the trees and building houses. He ran into opposition from the local council who wouldn't give him planning permission. He tried appealing but it did no good so on and off over the last five years he's been looking for someone to put in an offer for it. By the way Guv we are talking about someone who is now resident in Spain where he's made a fortune buying and selling apartments and villas. He recently put everything in the hands of an agent who I managed to catch up with yesterday afternoon – a chap named Pitkeathley based in Shrewsbury.'

'What did he have to say?'

'He told me he did a valuation of the woodland six months ago but he wasn't over-optimistic about finding a buyer prepared to pay the right price. He described the wood as neglected with work needing doing on repairing fences and removing dead trees He's hoping a conservation society might show some interest. Some of the oaks are hundreds of years old.'

'What about the theory of this being the work of some trigger-happy gamekeeper? Someone who came across Mattox in the process of trying to bag a few pheasants and took a pot shot at him?'

'He rubbished it straight away. First, no one to his knowledge has ever used the wood for rearing pheasants, certainly not in recent years, and second, according to him, his client isn't from the hunting, shooting, fishing fraternity.'

'No gamekeepers on patrol then?'

'No Guv.'

Just then Sergeant Hobbs put his head round the door.

'Sorry to interrupt gents but DI Millership is after a quick word with you Inspector. That is providing it's convenient.'

Moon muttered something under his breath audible only to Thompson who was sitting next to him.

'Thanks Mick,' he said to Sergeant Hobbs. 'Tell DI Millership I'll be with him shortly. We've almost finished here.'

***

Millership's ascendency to one of the top floor offices had been a pivotal moment in his career. Although the ultimate accolade of his own private lavatory had so far eluded him, he was still several steps up on anyone else who held his rank. Proof to Charlie Moon if it was needed that bowing and scraping brought rewards to those who did it.

Millership looked up when Moon walked in.

'Take a seat Charlie,' he said.

'Thanks,' said Moon pulling up a chair.

'I stopped off to see the boss last night,' Millership began. 'Naturally he's keen to make sure he's kept in the picture while he's off sick.'

'Naturally.' Moon had already got a mental picture of Millership going round to Willoughby's house carrying a bunch of grapes in one hand and a get well card in the other.

'He wants a full update on all current enquiries.' Moon couldn't make his mind up whether this really came from Willoughby or whether Millership was working on some agenda of his own.

'The case of the body in the woods. What's the latest?'

Experience had taught Moon to be careful when answering questions from Millership. He knew anything he said would be reported back to Willoughby.

'We're still trying to establish a motive. So far we've not found anything to link the victim to the place where he was found.'

'What stage are we at with the enquiry?'

'We're still asking round to see if anybody in the area has information to give. Mattox, the victim, came from Hereford and we might learn more about him from that end. We'll see.'

'I understand he has a criminal record.'

'Yes, he's been in a bit of bother over the years.'

'Could we be looking at a falling-out among thieves?'

'Perhaps. We're not ruling anything out.'

'So you don't see this as an open and shut case?'

Moon hesitated. He'd been caught out before getting drawn into saying too much to Millership. He decided to play safe.

'It's too early to call,' he replied.

Back in the makeshift incident room Moon took the opportunity to study the OS map Thompson had left taped to the whiteboard. Scott and Tamberlin had nipped off for a cup of coffee while Thompson was elsewhere making a phone call to Sergeant Kite in Hereford to see if one of Mattox's close associates would agree to a meeting. Up to now the associate in question had been playing hard to get but, according to Sergeant Kite, he was softening up mainly thanks to a reminder that life could get difficult if the police decided to take a more active interest in the disappearance of a skip full of scrap metal from a factory yard just after Christmas.

Though he had never sought to make it common knowledge, Charlie Moon had a natural talent for reading maps going back to his time in the Boy Scouts. In no time at all he could assemble contour lines and spot heights and transform them into three-dimensional pictures in his head. By doing this now he saw straight away Wrox Wood was on the side of a valley looking down on a village about a mile and a half away. In between lay fields with farms and small settlements dotted here and there. He picked out features such as the track of an old railway and a line of electricity transmission pylons crossing the valley from one side to the other. The village had a pub, a telephone box and a church with no spire. He searched for the little green symbols to denote where conifer trees grew and found the high ground on both sides of the valley covered in them. As to streams he found any number draining into the main watercourse which ran down the middle of the valley passing through the village. The main road, along which Moon had driven, bypassed the village.

His eyes drifted back to the red circle Thompson had drawn around the crime scene. He tried to imagine a fleeing man in shirtsleeves thrashing through the trees with an armed pursuer coming after him. The wood would offer a hiding place of sorts but not if the pursuer had the advantage of knowing the ground. Finally the moment of reckoning with the fleeing man cornered and pleading for mercy followed by two shots, first one then another, before silence reigned again and his body was left for the woodland creatures to pick over. Moon grimaced. A life of crime didn't always pay.

CHAPTER FOUR

A Place of Ghosts

A FEW WEEKS EARLIER

Tim's feet were not as bad as he feared. His ankles were rubbed but there was no sign of blisters. Still, he told himself as he prepared to leave the cottage the following day, best to take no chances. So, instead of his new boots, he put on an old pair of loafers he kept for driving. Today he would stick to walking on roads with the aim of going no further than a couple of miles.

It was just after ten when he set off. At the crossroads he went left towards the village which he could see still shrouded in mist in the distance. No one passed him except for a man on a motor bike going the other way. After about half a mile he came to a few scattered houses some of which looked shut up and empty. He noticed a bungalow on the left which stood on a small plot of land surrounded by bare arable fields. An old Suzuki van was parked on the front and beside it stood a woman staring down with a perplexed look on her face.

'Are you alright?' Tim called across. She didn't seem to hear him at first then she looked up and smiled. 'It's not my lucky day,' she said pointing to the flat tyre on the van's nearside.

Tim went over to take a closer look.

'I keep meaning to learn how to change a wheel,' she said. 'Sadly I've never managed to get round to it.'

Tim laughed.

'You can start by watching me,' he said then he took his coat off and laid it on the ground.

He guessed the woman was in her thirties, dressed casually yet smartly in a thick woollen jumper and blue jeans. She watched him as he worked, arms folded, one foot slightly in front of the other.

'There,' he said when he finished and showed her the rusty nail that had penetrated the tread of her tyre.

'There's a place on the industrial estate where I can get it fixed,' she said. 'I'll take it in later. It was kind of you to stop and help me.'

Tim took a tissue out of the small pack he always kept in his pocket and went to wipe his hands.

'Please,' she said. 'Come inside and use my bathroom.'

Tim followed her to the front door of the bungalow which was standing open. 'On the left,' she said pointing the way up a narrow hallway.

The bathroom looked like it had been recently modernised: a washbasin, a loo and a shower. There was a watercolour on the wall that could have been an original: deep purple hills in the distance looking down on meadows filled with wild flowers. He wondered whether she'd painted it herself and, if so, was it a scene from her imagination or somewhere she knew?

'I'm making coffee,' she called as he came out. Following the direction of her voice brought him to a small kitchen where she was busy grinding coffee beans.

He looked round. The kitchen was furnished in a rustic style with glass jars and cookery books on the shelves and herbs growing in pots on the window sills.

'I haven't seen you before,' she said over the noise of the coffee grinder. 'Are you new to these parts or just visiting?'

'I'm renting a place for a few weeks,' he replied. 'I may stay longer. It depends.'

She put the ground coffee into a filter machine and switched it on. 'It shouldn't take long,' she said. 'While we're waiting I'll show you my workshop.'

With that, she took him back down the narrow hallway and through a door that led into a large room with a low ceiling and windows on two sides. All around were trestle-tables, rolls of material, measuring tapes, scissors, dressmakers' patterns, reels of cotton and, over by one of the windows, a tailor's manikin next to an industrial-sized sewing machine.

'It's what I do,' she explained, picking up a card of buttons that had fallen on the floor.

'You make clothes.'

She smiled. 'That's the plan,' she said. 'When I make a name for myself. Right now I earn my crust by running up curtains, doing alterations, that kind of thing.'

'Is business good?'

'On and off,' she replied. 'I get most of my work from dress shops, tailors and dry cleaners. Just at the moment there's a call for letting out waistbands. Christmas dinners,' she explained with a smile pushing back a piece of hair that had fallen across her face. They went back into the kitchen where the coffee was almost ready. She took two mugs from a row of hooks on the wall.

'You've not said what you do.'

'My last job was in engineering,' he replied. 'I was made redundant at the end of last year. Right now I'm taking time out before I decide what I want to do next.'

'Which is what brought you here?'

'Partly.'

He studied her face as she poured the coffee. Pale, slender features with hardly a trace of make-up but striking in a way that was hard to describe.

'Have you thought about working for yourself?'

'It's one of the options but starting up on your own in engineering would call for a big capital outlay. Machine tools, premises, a whole range of costly items.'

'Does that put you off?'

He smiled. 'I'm not sure. Ask me in six months.'

A noise from outside drew her attention. She put her mug of coffee down and opened the window to let in a black cat.

'So where's this place you're renting?' she said picking up the cat and stroking it.

'Not far away. Turn right at the crossroads and it's the first cottage you come to. We're practically neighbours.'

She smiled again. 'In which case perhaps we should introduce ourselves. My name's Jen Mortimer.'

'Tim,' he replied 'Tim Stafford.'

He finished his coffee and thanked her.

'It's me who should be thanking you,' she said following him to the front door still holding the cat in her arms. 'I'll try to avoid driving over nails in future.'

As he walked off he turned round and looked back. She was still standing on the doorstep, still watching, still with the cat in her arms.

★★★

Next morning Tim set off early with the intention of exploring beyond the place where he'd met Joe Darby. This time he carried a rucksack and, as a precaution against his feet rubbing again, he put on an extra thick pair of socks. Into the rucksack he put a bag containing the sandwiches he'd made earlier and four small bottles of spring water.

When he reached the crossroads he turned right up the narrow sunken lane again then past the farm gate where the flock of sheep were still grazing in the field. He felt the wind on his face starting to freshen as he strode out and noticed dark threatening clouds gathering overhead. Still, it felt good to be out in the open air pleasing himself. He saw no one again and, when he came to the driveway with its big stone pillars and its stern warning notice, he went past without stopping. He came to where the lane turned into a track. Here he noticed the imprints of someone's boots in the mud but then he smiled to himself because he realised they were probably his own from two days before.

The track took him into the area of scattered woodland where he saw the trees were mainly stunted ashes and whitebeams. The track was following the foot of an escarpment but, as he trudged along, he saw no signs of anyone having used it for a long time. Just two deep ruts that could have been made by horse-drawn carts years ago.

Quarter of a mile further on he took a path to the left which climbed steeply. Soon the ashes and whitebeams gave way to an open downland dotted here and there with blackthorn bushes and spindle trees. The path carried on going up until finally it brought him to the crest of the ridge where a view over a broad and misty dale beyond opened up.

He stopped here to look back. Behind the path he'd just climbed and, further off, he could make out the twisting course of the lane, clear to see because of its twin line of overgrown hedgerows. He took the binoculars out of his pocket and brought the view into close-up picking out details such as the farm gate where he'd stood to look at the sheep. It occurred to him he might be able to see what lay beyond the big stone wall from up here but, when he pointed the binoculars in the right direction, he was disappointed. A haze drifted across the treetops that could have been smoke from a chimney but otherwise there was nothing to be seen.

The wind felt raw on the top of the ridge, chafing his cheeks, and, as he stood there, the first few drops of rain started to fall. A raven flew up, a black shape wheeling and flapping until it disappeared into the distance. Deciding to leave the path along the ridgeline for another day he slowly retraced his steps back to the ashes and the whitebeams until finally he came to the old cart road again. He checked his watch. It was too soon to think about eating his sandwiches so he carried on walking noticing the rain was starting to come down more heavily. Still, he told himself, no use worrying now. Besides, it would be a good test to see if his new coat was as waterproof as the manufacturers claimed.

Just as he was starting to wonder where the cart road was leading, his eyes caught sight of something up in front. A small brick building with a flat concrete roof on the far side of a level open space. He stopped walking. The building had no glass in its windows and a wooden door which was hanging off its hinges. It stood, he saw, at the entrance to an old limestone working quarried into the hillside. He took two steps forward then two steps more. Drawing level with the derelict building he paused briefly to take a look inside. Nothing apart from a heap of rubble and broken glass in the middle of the floor and the musty smell of damp and decay. Moss growing on the window sills and stains of black mildew creeping up the walls. He carried on walking into the quarry. To one side what looked like the remains of an old winch rusting away among the weeds while, overhead, towering rock faces looked down. An opaque milky-coloured pool pocked with raindrops filled the bottom of the quarry and he stood there staring at it while wondering how long it had been since this place had last been worked. Now there was nothing left except a hush everywhere. A place where the living no longer came. A place of ghosts.

CHAPTER FIVE

Jason Hemmings

A FEW WEEKS LATER

Though it was still early days, Moon's reading of the situation on the home front was that the bunch of flowers had done its job. Conversation over dinner had gone back more or less to normal but he knew all the same that he needed to be more mindful in future of upsetting domestic harmony by silly oversights.

Thompson drove as they headed off down the M5 in a heavy downpour with headlights on and windscreen wipers thrashing. They came off the motorway at just after ten then, following directions given to them by Sergeant Kite, they took a minor road passing cider mills, half-timbered farm buildings and converted oast houses.

'This is it,' said Moon pointing to a lay-by coming up on the left.

Thompson pulled over next to a large heap of frost grit. They were quarter of an hour early so they sat with the engine turned off listening to the rain drumming down on the roof. Traffic went by, throwing up spray, while Moon passed the time staring out of the side window at the hedge that had been turned into a fly-tippers' paradise.

'Looks like him,' said Thompson spotting the white transit van coming towards them with its indicator lights flashing. The van pulled up at the far end of the lay-by facing them. At first nothing happened then a man got out wearing a fleece over a white t-shirt and an old pair of jeans. The description given by Sergeant Kite fitted him perfectly. Jason Hemmings: one time associate of Sean Mattox: white male, early thirties, medium build, dark hair parted to one side and hanging down over his collar. Face, round and undistinguished looking apart from a small moustache. As the man got close enough Moon held his ID up to the windscreen.

It was Hemmings who had chosen the place for the meeting with the two detectives from Team Penda. Out of town and away from people who might want to know more about what he was doing talking to strangers who had the look of police. Though Hemmings had only been out in the rain briefly Moon immediately noticed the wet smell on his clothes as he slid into the back seat.

'I'm only here because of what's happened to Sean,' he quickly explained to make it clear it wasn't normal practice for him to be helping the law. Moon pulled down the sun visor and angled it so the vanity mirror gave him a clear view of Hemmings' face.

'Knew him long, did you?'

Hemmings broke off the eye contact. 'Three or four years. Depends what you call long.'

'When did you last see him?'

'Just after Christmas. He was in a pub in town and bought me a pint.'

'Was anyone with him?'

'No. He came in on his own.'

'What did you talk about?

'This and that. I hadn't seen him for weeks. It was mostly catching up.'

'Did he say where he was living?'

'I can't remember it coming up.'

'How did he appear? Relaxed? Agitated? Worried about anything?'

'Not that I could tell. He'd just won fifty quid on a horse.'

'Was he a gambling man?'

'He wasn't in and out of the betting shop, if that's what you mean. He went to race meetings a lot. He always said it was a place he got to meet interesting people.'

'Did he have any enemies? People who bore him a grudge?'

'No one I can think of. No one who'd go as far as shooting him.'

'What about girlfriends?'

'What about them?'

'Was he seeing anyone?'

'Search me boss. He didn't tell me his secrets.'

'There's a rumour doing the rounds he was living with a woman.'

'It didn't come from me.'

Moon decided to try a different tack.

'Mr Hemmings it's been suggested to us that Sean may have been mixed up in poaching. What would be your reading of that?'

Hemmings shook his head. 'I'd say it was bollocks. There are people in town who go poaching but Sean wasn't one of them.'

'So if he didn't run into an angry gamekeeper what would be your guess on what happened to him?'

'Straight up?

'Straight up.'

Hemmings fidgeted with his fingers, took his time to answer in the manner of someone thinking carefully about what they're going to say next.

'I'd put my money on him biting off more than he could chew. Got into something he couldn't handle.'

'Is there any reason you're saying this?'

Hemmings looked up, made eye contact in the mirror briefly then looked away again.

'When I saw him in the pub he said something that stuck in my mind. By then he'd knocked back a few jars and Sean was never one for holding his drink.'

'Go on.'

'He was talking about a big job he was planning. Not here in Hereford. Somewhere else but he wouldn't say where.'

'Was that it?'

'More or less. He said he was branching out, trying his hand at something different. Talked about all the money he was going to make.'

'What did you make of it?'

'At first I could only think of drugs.'

'Did that surprise you?'

'Yeah it did. You might catch Sean smoking a spliff occasionally but he always said dealing in drugs was a mug's game.'

'So if it wasn't drugs, what else do you think he might have had his fingers in?'

'My guess is as good as yours boss.'

'Can you recall anything more he said? Anything that might give us a lead into what was going on in his life?'

Hemmings fidgeted with his fingers again. 'Just as I left him he made some crack about the next time I saw him he'd be driving a Porsche.'

'Did you take him seriously?'

'At the time no. I put it down to the drink talking. I wish now I'd pumped him a bit more.'

'I'm sorry I've not been much help,' Hemmings said as he got out into the rain.

Moon wound down his side window. 'You may have stopped us chasing up a few blind alleys.'

Hemmings nodded. 'I hope you catch the bastard who did it,' he said.

'So do I Mr Hemmings.'

Just as the man in the fleece was making his way back to the transit van Moon called over to him.

'Keep your ear to the ground, Mr Hemmings. If you hear anything interesting let us know.'

'I will,' said Hemmings raising his hand.

As Moon and Thompson made their way back to the motorway neither of them spoke for a while.

'Any thoughts Guv?' said Thompson as they joined the tailback of traffic which had built up behind a farm tractor.

'Not really,' said Moon keeping his eyes on the line of cars in front.

'Did you buy that stuff about Mattox getting ideas above his station?'

'I didn't think Hemmings was trying to pull the wool over our eyes, if that's what you mean.' The farm tractor turned off into a field and the line of cars started to pick up speed.

'So where's all this going?' said Thompson as he changed up through the gears.

'Nowhere quickly,' said Moon.

***

Next morning Charlie Moon woke in a cold sweat.

He knew he'd been dreaming but the dream was so real it took a few seconds to adjust. He'd been walking in a forest; trees, trees and more trees going on and on and never coming to an end. Then the cry that broke the dream, a cry that came from nowhere but at the same time was all around him. A cry for help. A cry like the cry of a frightened child.

He got out of bed on the pretext of going to the bathroom but he knew what he really wanted to do was go and see the girls were alright. Cathy stirred in her sleep as he shuffled his feet round on the carpet to find his slippers. The girls' bedroom doors were both open and he checked inside. Two heads resting peacefully on their pillows, he tip-toed away carefully so as not to disturb them.

It was just after five and, seeing no point in going back to bed for another hour, he took himself off downstairs. He took Cathy a cup of tea before he left then spent five minutes scraping ice off the car windows. The morning traffic was already starting to build up. A grey light in the sky over to the east, he turned the car heater onto full blast to stop the windscreen misting up.

His journey took him across a landscape where foundries and tube mills had once stood but where property developers' signs now proclaimed a brave new world of retail parks, entertainment complexes and shopping malls. He flicked the radio on to catch the weather report. A warm front coming in from the west. It would be turning mild and wet after a chilly start.

Sergeant Hobbs gave him the bad news the IT systems were up and running again. Moon made no comment. Instead he carried on walking but, once in the office, he stared at the one-eyed monster sitting on the desk and muttered a few choice words under his breath. He knew it wouldn't be long before Willoughby would be back on line with nothing better to do than fire off emails calling for information on this, that or the other. The thought of it filled him with gloom.

It was just after eleven when Thompson put his head round the door.

'Can I have a word Guv?' he said.

Thompson had been going through the list of licensed shotgun owners on the off-chance one or other of them had crossed paths with the law at some time in the past.

'All squeaky clean until I came to this character,' said Thompson holding up a foolscap pad on which he'd jotted down some notes. 'Name: Williams. Forenames: Leinthall O'Rourke. Date of birth: 9.06.1947. He was arrested in North Wales five years ago charged with rape. The case came up in Mold Crown Court in 1997 but then it was dropped. Williams now lives about two and a half miles from where Mattox's body was found.'

Moon took the foolscap pad from him. Thompson meanwhile carried on talking.

'Earlier on I spent the best part of an hour trying to track down one of the officers who'd been involved in the case. In the end I was put through to a DS Crombie who was a member of the original investigating team. At first I thought she was being cagey with me but then she explained what happened in 1997 was a sore point with her and her colleagues. The trial collapsed on its second day and Williams walked off scot-free. What I'm guessing is the police were left with egg on their faces.'

'And what I'm guessing is DS Crombie had her arse kicked and doesn't want reminding about it. Is that all?'

'I tried pushing her to tell me more but she seemed reluctant. It was like…'

'Like what?'

'Like she'd been warned off. Like the subject of Williams was taboo.'

Moon sat for a while after Thompson left. The sensible side of his head was telling him to check his emails but, as history repeatedly showed, the sensible side of Charlie Moon's head didn't always prevail. Instead he found his eyes kept drifting back to the foolscap pad still sitting on the desk where Thompson left it. Williams. Leinthall O'Rourke. Charge of rape. He went over to the door to make sure it was closed before tapping a number into the keypad of his mobile phone. The line connected and, after three rings, a familiar voice answered.

Charlie Moon hadn't spoken to Jo Lyon for over six months. Jo earned her living as a freelance journalist writing mostly on women's issues and she and Moon went back to the day he stood next to her in a second-hand record shop browsing through old American vinyls. Jo was in the city centre when she picked up Moon's call and, when he explained he didn't want to talk over the phone, they agreed to meet for an early evening drink in a pub they both knew.

They found a quiet table in a corner well away from the gaggle of smokers who were standing by the bar.

'This must be my lucky day,' said Jo taking the first sip from her glass of wine. 'An exclusive interview with the city's top cop. Tell me what I've done to deserve this great honour.'

Moon handed over the Lowell Fulson box set. Jo smiled, partly in appreciation and partly because he'd left the price on it.

'So what's the real reason you've got me here?' she said after she'd run her eyes approvingly over the track list. 'On the phone it sounded like you'd got something hush-hush you wanted to talk about.'

'Does the name Leinthall Williams mean anything to you?'

'No. Why should it?'

'He was charged with rape in North Wales back in 1997. He got off and I want to know what happened.'

'So why are you asking me?'

'I admit it's a long shot Jo. Williams' name has cropped up in an investigation and I want to know more about him.'

'I still don't understand why you're asking me. Surely the police in North Wales have all the answers.'

Moon pulled a face. 'We tried them but it didn't get us very far. Yes, I know I could go through official channels but I'd rather know what I could be getting into first.'

'Do you smell a rat?'

'At this stage I'm not sure.'

The pub was starting to fill up with after work drinkers: men and women in business suits stopping off to relax and unwind before they made the trip home.

Jo spoke. 'So let me get this straight Charlie. You want me to ask round to see if anyone knows about this Williams' case?'

Moon nodded. 'I know four years is a long time ago but I'd appreciate it if you could put your ear to the ground. Anything you manage to dig up will help. Even if it's only to eliminate Williams from our enquiries.'

'Is he a suspect?'

'It's too early to say.'

'Charlie, am I entitled to know what this is all about?'

'Some small-time petty crook was found murdered near where Williams now lives.'

'Naturally you want your name kept out of it.'

'Please.'

Moon walked Jo back to her car. A fine drizzle had set in painting a wet scene outside on the streets. The warm weather front had arrived.

'I'll be in touch,' she said as she slipped into the driver's seat of the little Fiat.

'Thanks Jo,' he said then watched her as she drove off into the night.

Moon glanced at his watch. It was quarter to seven and briefly it went through his mind to go back to the office and check his emails. He stood for a while with his coat collar turned up running his eye along the line of cars parked in the street to see if he recognised any of the number plates.

Going back to HQ meant driving in the opposite direction to home and the prospect of Cathy with a long face when he walked through the door at half past eight. No, he said to himself, emails would have to wait.

CHAPTER SIX

Strange Happenings in the Night

A FEW WEEKS EARLIER

The rain started to come more steadily as Tim turned away from the quarry. He toyed briefly with the idea of taking shelter in the derelict building while he ate his sandwiches but there was something about the place which made him feel he didn't want to stay there any longer. He looked at his watch. He'd been out for just under two hours and, despite the rain, he didn't want to go back just yet. A path leading into the trees. He decided to take it to see where it went. Soon the ashes and whitebeams grew denser and the path became harder to follow. Here and there he came across pits in the ground overgrown with brambles: evidence of old limekilns, he wondered. A flock of wood pigeons flew up making flapping noises with their wings but otherwise the woods were silent apart from the sound of the wind and the soft pitter-patter of rain falling on the leaf mould.

He trudged on, his hair slowly getting more and more soaked while his new coat did a good job of keeping the rest of him dry. All traces of the path he'd been following had vanished and he found himself going this way then that hoping and praying the general direction he was taking would bring him out somewhere.

Finally he came to where the woodland gave way to straight rows of tall conifer trees which went off into the distance. There was no fence line or anything else to say the plantation was someone's private property so he kept going noticing how the conifers shut out more and more of the light from the sky. Beneath his feet a carpet of pine needles while above his head he could hear the wind cutting through the treetops. An eerie stillness all around him broken only by the sound of rain dripping from the branches and twigs snapping under his boots. Here and there he had to duck down under overhanging branches. He had no idea where he was going. The lines of tree trunks looked the same in every direction, in front, behind and on both sides. It crossed his mind more than once he could be walking round in circles.

After ten minutes he stopped. Checking his watch again he saw it was just over three quarters of an hour since he left the quarry and his thoughts turned to finding somewhere to sit down and eat. He noticed a fallen tree and took his sandwiches and one of the bottles of water out of his rucksack. As he sat there taking in the mix of damp resiny smells, he caught sight of something out of the corner of his eye. A shape. A grey outline standing among the tree trunks but, when he looked again, it was gone.

It took him twenty minutes to find his way back to the ashes and whitebeams then, more by luck than by judgment, he came out again on the old cart road. The rain had slackened off but parts of the cart road which had been muddy before had turned into a quagmire. He picked his way round the worst bits and soon he found himself back where the track gave way to the hard paved surface of the lane. Over to the left, he could see the big wall behind its screen of bushes while the lane itself was already awash with rain water. He carried on walking, splashing through the puddles.

He was coming up to the gate with its stark warning notice when he caught sight of something which made him stop. A large dog, a mastiff by the looks of it, he hadn't noticed it at first but it was standing on the other side of the cattle grid, perfectly still and watching him. Tim hesitated. Was this the same dog Joe Darby had warned him about? He had no idea but its jaws looked powerful enough to tear flesh to shreds.

The mastiff started pacing, going up and down along the edge of the cattle grid like a caged animal. All muscle and sinew with pricked up ears and a scarred snout. Tim edged forward deciding to put his trust in the cattle grid doing its job and keeping the dog on the far side. He wished though he'd thought to pick up a stick or something else he could defend himself with if he needed to but it was too late to worry about such things now. He was getting closer to the dog, never once taking his eyes off it and noticing the unpleasant way it kept baring its teeth. Don't show fear, an inner voice kept telling him. Don't make sudden movements and don't be a fool and try to make a run for it. He came level with the driveway, turning his head to one side to keep the mastiff in his peripheral vision and almost falling over his feet as he did. Suddenly the mastiff stopped pacing and, for one heart-stopping moment, Tim thought it was going to pounce. Instead it started barking, so loud Tim half-expected to see someone come running down the drive to find out what all the fuss was about. He quickened his pace, glancing over his shoulder every so often. The dog was still there, still behind the cattle grid, still barking, until finally he lost sight of it round a bend in the lane.

***

Back at the cottage he changed out of his wet trousers and hung his coat up to dry. Sitting in front of a log fire with a mug of tea and a plate of hot buttered pikelets, soon he was starting to feel drowsy and, before he knew it, he'd fallen into a deep and dreamless sleep.

He woke with a start and noticed straight away the rain had stopped and it had gone dark outside. He checked his watch. It was just after seven and, by his own reckoning, he'd been asleep for four hours.

Still feeling full after the pikelets, he decided to go out and stretch his legs to work up an appetite. His coat still felt damp so he decided to brave the cold by wearing just the thick winter woolly he'd changed into earlier.

He let himself out of the front door and noticed the stars in the sky and the cold frosty chill of the night air. An old moon was sinking over to the west and there was a fresh smell to everything after the morning's rain.

He decided to take a slow walk up to the crossroads with the idea of, when he got there, turning round and coming back. There was no wind and the stillness was broken only by the sound of water trickling in the ditch.

When he reached the crossroads he saw a few lights twinkling down in the village. He stood there for a while staring up at the constellations, his eyes gradually getting more and more used to the dark. He shivered but, just as he was about to make his way back to the cottage, something made him stop.

Headlights. At first they seemed a long way off but, as he watched, they started to get closer. They were coming towards him from the direction of the village, up the lane past the scattering of dwellings where Jen Mortimer lived. Soon he picked up the noise of a car engine crawling along in low gear but something told him not to stay out here in the open where anybody could see him. A big holly bush beckoned, standing on a corner of the crossroads with just enough space behind it to hide. The headlights were coming closer, close enough to start casting pale shadows along the banks and hedgerows. He drew back further into the tight space behind the holly bush craning his neck to catch a glimpse of who had chosen to make the trip to this lonely place after dark. A large 4x4, a top of the range job, with two men sitting in the front and three more in the back. He could hear their voices but the noise of the 4x4's engine made it impossible to tell what they were saying. The 4x4 paused at the crossroads just a few yards away from his hiding place then it moved off again but instead of going left or right, it went straight on up the narrow sunken lane which, as Tim now knew, was the way to nowhere apart from whatever lay behind the big stone wall. But soon Tim was in for another surprise. A second 4x4 was following the first and a third close behind.

He stayed in his hiding place behind the holly bush

until he could hear the noise of the 4x4s' engines growing fainter but, just when he thought it was safe to come out, another sound reached his ears. A car again but this time the deep throbbing sound of a souped-up engine followed by the steady thump thump thump of loud music being pumped through giant speakers. He drew back again into the prickly foliage and waited. The car had stopped at the crossroads and, peeping out so he could get a better look, Tim could make out a man wearing a baseball cap pulled down over his eyes behind the driving wheel and someone else sitting in the passenger seat. The car, he saw, was an old Ford Escort, its colour impossible to make out in the dark, but judging by how the driver kept pointing, it seemed he was trying to work out which way to go. Seconds passed. Finally the Escort moved off up the sunken lane going in the same direction as the 4x4s but, as it went past, Tim saw it had a white circle painted on the side on which someone had stencilled the number seven.

***

The strange procession of cars made Tim's mind go back to the conversation with Joe Darby. Poachers, people who probably went about their business after dark and who wouldn't take too kindly to anyone observing what they were doing. It was a coincidence therefore that, the following morning just as Tim was getting ready to go out of the front gate, the old man with eyes that missed nothing came walking by with Jack the fox terrier scampering at his heels.

'It don't sound like poachers to me,' said Joe after he

listened to what Tim had to say. 'Besides I know every poacher in a ten mile radius of here and not one of them has got the kind of car you've just described. Old clapped-out vans more like it.'

Tim told him about the boy racer in the Ford Escort with his woofers turned up full blast.

'That settles it for me,' said Joe taking off his cap to scratch the top of his head. 'No self-respecting poacher would be letting everyone know he was coming by making a lot of noise. No, sounds more to me like someone with business up at the top of the lane.'

'The place with the wall round it?'

'There's nowhere else up the top of the lane.'

'Do you know who lives there?'

'A chappie who bought the place last year,' Joe replied. 'He's already rubbed up a few people the wrong way. Not me, you understand, because I've never spoken to him but some who've crossed paths with him wish they hadn't.'

'What's his problem?'

'No manners,' said Joe. 'Take what happened to Bob Preece as an example. Bob is one of the nicest people you could wish to meet and his family have farmed round here for six generations. Back in October Bob was moving some of his sheep to fresh grazing which meant he had to drive them up the lane. Just as he was doing it with one of his sons helping along comes his lordship in his big Range Rover. First he starts blowing his horn then out he gets and has a go at Bob calling him all sorts of names including peasant. Bob couldn't believe his ears but by then his son had got the sheep through the gate into the field where they were going and our friend got back in his car and drove off. From that day to this Bob has made a point of keeping out of his way.'

Tim watched Joe as he walked off towards the crossroads. Soon he lost sight of him.

***

Next day Tim drove into town to stock up on provisions. He set off just before twelve, turned left at the crossroads and went past the bungalow where Jen Mortimer lived. There was no sign of the Suzuki van but he did notice the black cat sitting outside the front door. When he came to the main road he went right and covered the short distance into town in ten minutes. He parked on what looked like it had once been a cattle market and, as he did, he noticed a few spots of rain starting to fall. Rather than get wet again so soon after his last soaking he decided to look for somewhere to have lunch.

The town still had an after Christmas look to it with sale signs in the shop windows and a few people out looking for bargains. He found a pub called The King's Arms where he sat under a low beamed ceiling eating home-made fish pie, drinking a pint of local farmhouse cider and listening to the soft burr of country voices drifting through from the bar.

Back on the streets again he did the shopping he needed to do then, as the rain had eased off and, with nothing more pressing on his mind, he decided to take a look round. Continuing along the High Street, he noticed how the buildings took on a more run-down appearance the further he got from the town centre. The country outfitters, the antique dealers and the delis gave way to a betting office, a shop selling cheap furniture and several premises with their windows boarded up. He stopped outside a place renting videos where it crossed his mind a movie might make a change from watching the standard offering on the telly.

Inside the shop was empty apart from a man sitting behind a counter at the far end smoking a cigarette. All around the walls were cases of videos arranged in categories and Tim spent the next five minutes browsing through them. He came to a section marked 'Adult' where he paused. The man behind the counter spoke.

'You might find what you're looking for through there,' he said taking the cigarette from his lips and pointing to where an old curtain was drawn across a doorway.

★★★

It was dark when Tim got back. As soon as he walked in he switched on the oven then spent the next ten minutes preparing the ingredients for a pot-au-feu. Once dinner was slowly cooking he opened the bottle of Nuits-St-Georges he'd bought in town and put it on the table to breathe. He then went outside to fetch two logs for the fire from the stack against the wall by the back door. Down the garden path the remains of the old greenhouse and the rusty wheelbarrow tipped over on its side among the weeds. He heard the owl again and, faintly in the distance, the sound of traffic on the main road.

After dinner he sat on one of the two comfy sofas in front of the fire listening to the damp logs hissing and crackling and sending showers of sparks up the chimney. He helped himself to another glass of wine. The video was already in the machine waiting.

At first a long warning scrolled up the screen about infringing film-maker's rights and the penalties awaiting those who did. He pressed fast-forward then play again. This time he found himself looking at titles in a language he didn't understand. He fast-forwarded the tape further to a scene where two men in flared trousers looking like seventies' throwbacks were chatting up a blonde. The soundtrack was dubbed, the picture grainy and the blonde had just agreed to go with the two men for a swim in the sea. Cut to a beach where the blonde and one of the men were writhing naked in the sand. Tim yawned. Soon he was fast asleep.

It was after midnight when he woke up. The video had finished long ago and the screen in front of him was flickering. He searched for the remote control and found it down the side of the cushion he was sitting on. Pressing the rewind button he waited for the tape to track back but just as he was returning it to its case something fell out on the floor. A small printed card like a business card. He picked it up and read it. There was the name 'Mandy' and underneath in small letters the words 'massage, relaxation, escort services' followed by a mobile phone number.

CHAPTER SEVEN

Revenge is a Dangerous Game

A FEW WEEKS LATER

'Got a minute Charlie?' The voice on the other end of the line belonged to Millership. The call came so soon after Moon got in that it was clear that Willoughby's unofficial number two had been waiting for him to arrive.

'Sure,' said Moon feigning nonchalance while his mind went into overdrive going through all the possible reasons why Millership would be wanting to see him again so soon. Top of the list was the meeting in the pub with Jo Lyon and the instruction he'd been given two years ago not to have any dealings with the media before clearing it with Willoughby first. Was this dirty tricks again? Willoughby and Millership doing what they'd done before and having him followed? Moon tried to bring back to mind the faces in the pub. The early evening drinkers, the gaggle of girls who came in looking like they were on their way to a hen party, the man in the corner sitting on his own reading a newspaper over a pint of beer.

He stopped off in the gents to straighten his tie as was his habit when feeling the need to be on his best mettle. It certainly wasn't done out of any compulsion to smarten up his appearance for the sake of a worm like Millership.

'Thanks for coming up,' said Millership with his characteristic oily smoothness as Moon walked in without knocking. The grey-suited figure was sitting at his desk filling his gold fountain pen with ink. 'Sorry if I interrupted anything Charlie but the boss has asked me to speak to you about the emails he's been sending.'

'Emails?' Moon affected the totally blank expression he kept for moments like these.

'The boss has been sending you emails,' said Millership putting the top back on the bottle of ink. 'He's concerned you may not have received them.'

'The system's been down,' said Moon continuing to look blank.

Millership cleared his throat. 'The boss is referring to emails he's sent you since the system's been back up. Are you saying you've not seen them?'

'Definitely not,' said Moon telling what was after all the truth but pleased that Millership was handling this interrogation not Willoughby who would have seen through the deception straight away. Moon then ended the conversation by saying he'd get someone from IT to go over his PC as a matter of priority.

Afterwards he felt pleased with himself for putting one over on Millership but a warning voice was telling him to be more careful in future. Willoughby had a bee in his bonnet about officers checking their emails and being flippant about it was a sure way of landing himself in trouble.

Moon's next stop was the small conference room where Thompson and Tamberlin were already in session. Scott was on a day's leave so Tamberlin was doing all the talking. The subject was the state of enquiries on the ground.

'It's exactly what you'd expect,' Tamberlin was saying. 'A quiet backwater. Nothing ever happens there apart from the odd teenager getting into trouble.'

'We've heard all this before Tambo,' said Moon tapping his fingers impatiently.

'I know Guv. But what are we expected to do? Turn up criminals when there aren't any?'

'What about the village bobby?' said Moon. 'With all due respect to Scotty and you, you're a couple of city boys when what we need is someone with their roots in the community; someone who knows the dodgy characters lurking behind the haystacks and what they get up to.'

Thompson interrupted. 'I made the same point Guv. Scotty and Tambo are prime targets for being led up the garden path.'

'So?'

'The village bobby got the chop in a round of spending cuts last year. He took early retirement and went off to live in Thailand. So far we haven't been able to trace him.'

Tamberlin spoke again. 'We've talked to all the usual people who get to hear the gossip. The landlord of the pub, the postman, the couple who run the village shop, the story with all of them is exactly the same. Total shock. Things like that don't happen round here.'

'Okay,' said Moon. 'Let's move on to the place where the body was found. A few acres of neglected woodland belonging to some bloke who hasn't visited it for years. Who goes there? Who goes up and down the lane? Can anybody recall seeing anything unusual going on?'

'Scotty and I had a word with the farmer whose land borders the wood,' Tamberlin replied. 'According to him there's not a lot of traffic uses the lane. There have been issues with fly-tippers going back to last Spring when the council stopped collecting garden rubbish.'

'What about the wood itself?'

'Sorry Guv…'

'What did this farmer friend of yours have to say about people who go there? Apart from picking bluebells what kind of things do they get up to?'

Tamberlin nodded. 'When we mentioned dogging he didn't know what we were talking about until Scotty explained.'

'Any reaction?'

'He laughed his head off. He said he had no idea such things went on.'

'Has he seen anything else?'

'In the time frame we're talking about? He couldn't recall anything out of the ordinary. He was mending a fence by the wood around the time we think Mattox was murdered. He can't recall hearing anyone shooting. He only became aware something had happened when he saw the police activity in the lane. The farmhouse where he lives is over half a mile away so Scotty and I came away feeling he wasn't covering anything up.'

'What about the old boy who found the body? What did he have to say for himself?'

'He was out walking his dog. He lives in the village but he goes up that way regularly. He took a turn through the wood taking the path he usually goes along. The dog ran off in front and the next minute he heard it barking.

When he went to see what it was about he came across Mattox's corpse half hidden under a pile of leaves and looking to him like the foxes had been at it. Fortunately he had a phone on him so the police were on the scene quickly.'

'On his walks has he noticed anyone acting suspiciously? Strangers? People he doesn't normally see?'

'He says he hardly ever claps eyes on anyone. The odd car goes by but he rarely sees people out on foot. He confirmed what the farmer had to say about fly-tippers. He reported a case himself. A jobbing gardener dumping a load of tree prunings.'

Moon rested the tips of his fingers on his temples. 'We don't seem to be getting very far,' he said. 'Leads so far, nil. Suspects, nil also. Clues to possible motives, we haven't fucking got any or is it me missing something? Sorry Tambo, I'm not getting at you but this is starting to look like a load of dead ends.'

Moon rarely used expletives and both Thompson and Tamberlin grinned.

'There's this Williams character,' said Thompson. 'He may not rank highly as a suspect but he ticks a few of the boxes.'

'Who's Williams?' said Tamberlin who hadn't been brought up to speed yet on Thompson's conversation with North Wales Police. Thompson quickly filled him in.

'I'm sure we've not spoken to anyone named Williams,' Tamberlin said flicking through the pages of his notebook.

'Dave, can we come back to Williams another time?'

Moon interjected. 'I've put out a few private lines of enquiry into his background but I want to keep it quiet – you know the score.'

'Sure Guv,' said Thompson knowing Moon had sources of information he kept to himself.

After the meeting broke up Moon nipped out to buy a baguette for his lunch. On the way back Sergeant Hobbs stopped him.

'There's some news,' he said. 'Mr Willoughby has been signed off by the doctor and he'll back on Monday.'

Moon switched on the one-eyed monster as soon as he got back in the office. The emails people had sent since the system was up and running started trickling through. They included three from Willoughby, the first despatched forty eight hours previously with a simple request to be updated on progress with the Mattox case. The other two were follow-ups, the last was noticeably tetchy in its tone, asking for a reply as a matter of urgency. Moon grimaced. This would probably mean he was in for a roasting the minute Willoughby came back on the scene. He knew, more to the point, he only had himself to blame. He ran through a range of excuses he could offer but, in the end, he had to admit none of them were very plausible. He wondered about saying his PC had developed a temporary fault which had now miraculously rectified itself. Willoughby, however, was notoriously red hot when it came to IT and trying to pull the wool over his eyes with technical stuff was asking for trouble. In the end Moon settled for replying by saying he was sorry and not going into detail. He drafted a form of words consistent with the line he'd fed to Millership about nothing coming to light yet that connected Mattox with where his body had been found. He kept it brief then, after he'd read it through a few times, he clicked the send button.

Moon spent the weekend running the girls round and, in between, fixing a fence in the garden which had been blown down by the wind. He thought keeping busy might keep his mind off Willoughby but it didn't and, once or twice, he found his attention drifting off when he was supposed to be listening to what Cathy was saying.

Monday morning came round all too quickly. Moon got in just after seven and, to his relief, there was no sign of either Willoughby or Millership – in fact the car park was almost empty.

He made it his first job to check his emails again knowing Willoughby had a habit of firing off edicts from his laptop on Sunday afternoons. Thankfully there was nothing and Moon turned his thoughts to having one of his periodic blitzes on the piles of paperwork that had built up on his desk. He kept his eyes on the car park through the slatted blinds of his office window. Millership arrived at quarter past eight and Willoughby drove in ten minutes later. He imagined Willoughby had more important tasks on his first morning back than holding the soles of his least favoured detective inspector's feet to the flames of the fire. Besides he would probably be spending his first hour closeted with Millership listening to all the gossip about what had been going on in his absence.

It was just after ten when the call from Jo came through.

'I'll come to you,' he said when she explained she had some information to pass on and an arrangement was made to meet for lunch in the city centre. The venue they chose was a tapas bar which was conveniently located in a quiet back street.

As he drove off Moon glanced up at the row of windows on the top floor. Willoughby had his blinds drawn to shut out the morning sun. Out on the street Moon made his customary check of the lines of parked cars. Some he recognised as belonging to HQ staff who hadn't been able to find a space on site. He kept his eyes glued on the rear-view mirror. No one pulled out behind him but, just to be on the safe side, he went off in the opposite direction to the city centre and drove around in circles until he was satisfied no one was following.

When he arrived at the tapas bar he spotted Jo's Fiat parked outside on a meter. She was already seated at a table when he walked in.

'Smile,' she said seeing the look on his face. 'You might feel better if you lightened up a bit.'

They ordered food and Jo chose the wine. As soon as the waiter went off Jo lost no time getting down to business.

'This case in North Wales,' she began. 'I've spoken to someone I've known for years named Stephanie Holt. Steph runs a rape victims' support group based in Chester. She recognised Williams' name straight away. The case you want to know about involved a girl from Wrexham named Vicky Rodericks who was just seventeen at the time. Back in the day Vicky would have been described as backward. She can't read or write and, in terms of her mental age, she is roughly at the level of a nine year old. Not surprisingly she found it hard to get a job when she left school. Finally a contract cleaning company agreed to give her a chance.'

'She worked as a cleaner?'

'Correct.'

'So where does Williams come in?'

'When all this happened he was living in big house out in the country not far from Wrexham. He paid the contract cleaners to go in twice a week, more often if he was entertaining.'

'This girl Vicky cleaned Williams' house?'

'Not on her own. There was another cleaner, an older woman, who was tasked with looking after her.'

The waiter came with the bottle of wine and Jo asked him to pour it. When he'd gone she carried on talking.

'It came out later the older woman was in the habit of nipping off early leaving Vicky to finish off on her own. Sometimes Williams was in the house, sometimes he wasn't. It didn't take him long though to seize his opportunity.'

'How many times did it happen?'

'Steph said it went on over a period of three months. By all accounts some of it was pretty brutal.'

'Vicky didn't tell anybody?'

'She was too scared of losing her job.'

'So how did it come out?'

'She became moody, withdrawn, to such an extent her family noticed. In the end she told her sister and her sister went straight to the police.'

'Do you know what Williams had to say for himself?'

'Denied it all, just as you'd expect. He said Vicky made things up and accused her of being deceitful.'

'What about forensic tests?'

'They took swabs, went over Vicky's clothing for traces of semen. According to the lab report nothing showed up but there was suspicion later someone hadn't done their job properly.'

'The tests were botched?'

'I think so but according to Steph it was all covered up.'

'So the prosecution case rested entirely on Vicky's evidence?'

'That's right. Williams' defence team did everything they could to get the charge dropped but the trial went ahead mainly because the police felt confident Vicky would make a credible witness.'

'Did she?'

'Sadly no. Williams hired a top London barrister who soon had her tied her up in knots. She contradicted herself so many times it became pitiful to watch.'

'Your friend Steph was there?'

'Yes. She was furious. She has been campaigning for years to stop rape victims having to face up to the ordeal of lengthy cross-questionings. That's what happened to Vicky – and, of course, she was too innocent to see when she was being led into traps. To make matters worse she had Williams staring at her from the dock all the time she was giving evidence.'

'The prosecution threw in the towel?'

Jo nodded. 'What you've been told is correct. The trial collapsed on its second day. By then poor Vicky was distraught. Worst of all, she thought she'd let everyone down: her mum and dad, her sister, the rest of her family and all the other people who'd supported her including the police.'

'Was Steph critical of the police?'

'On the contrary she was full of praise for the investigating team who were as angry as everyone else with the outcome. Steph said Williams left the court with a nasty smirk on his face. Afterwards there were rumours that he and some of his pals had a celebration at a nightclub cum lap dancing place somewhere in Manchester. What upset everybody most though was what happened later when the police had to pay Williams compensation. A large sum of money was involved. Steph doesn't know the details. It was all done behind closed doors.'

'What about Vicky?'

'As you'd expect, she was never the same again. Before she was happy-go-lucky, made friends, now she won't even go out of the house. She's scared she could bump into Williams.'

The food arrived and for a while they sat there eating in silence. Jo was first to speak.

'Charlie, have I told you anything that will help get Williams put behind bars?'

Moon looked at her. 'On a count of cold-blooded murder? Probably not.'

'Raping someone with the mind of a child is as low as it gets. Vicky didn't have much going for her in the first place but, whatever she did have, Williams has taken it away.'

'We live in a nasty world Jo. People like Williams are everywhere. With Vicky the damage has been done and there's nothing any of us can do to put it right.'

'But there is such a thing as payback?'

Moon smiled at her. 'Revenge is a dangerous game,' he replied.

They left the tapas bar separately. As soon as he was back on the streets Moon lost no time switching his phone back on only to find no voicemail messages or missed calls. He mingled with the crowds, studied reflections in shop windows and turned round occasionally to look who was behind. Never the same face twice. Just plain ordinary people going about their plain ordinary business.

Back at HQ Willoughby's car hadn't moved, neither had Millership's. The blinds to Willoughby's office were still drawn even though the sun had gone in a long time ago.

Sergeant Hobbs looked up as he walked in.

'Anyone been after me?' Moon asked.

Sergeant Hobbs shook his head. 'Not to my knowledge,' he replied.

The one-eyed monster took its time opening up only to reveal when it did that there was nothing new from upstairs. Was it strange? Willoughby had been back over half a day and not a single phone call or email. Moon's thoughts went back to the last time it all went quiet on the Willoughby front. Two years ago and the game of cat-and-mouse culminating in the day Willoughby pounced and he, Charlie Moon, came within a hair's breadth of becoming history. Was that what Willoughby was doing now? Watching and waiting for an opportunity to present itself? Moon was sure he'd soon be finding out. The worst part was the uncertainty.

CHAPTER EIGHT

The Minder

A FEW WEEKS EARLIER

The card was still on the top of the video player where Tim had left it when he went to bed the night before. Mandy, massage, relaxation, escort services: he found his eyes kept drifting back.

It was eleven o'clock in the morning and he was drinking a cup of strong coffee in front of the dying embers of the log fire. He reached for his wallet and counted out the notes. Eighty pounds in twenties plus another five from his trouser pocket in loose change. He had no idea how much working girls charged but, out here in the country, he figured it would be a lot less than in the city.

He picked up the phone, held it in the palm of his hand for a while and almost put it down again. Finally he tapped in the string of numbers he read off the card then waited for the line to connect. At first it went straight onto voicemail so he left it five minutes then tried again. This time a woman's voice answered.

'I came across one of your cards….,' he began then felt his mouth run dry as he searched for the right words to say.

'Give me your address,' she said. The accent was local and he could hear the sound of a television in the background. 'Is two o'clock this afternoon okay?' He said it was then the phone went down.

The time passed slowly. He found a few jobs to do and it went through his mind more than once to ring up again and cancel the whole thing. Two o'clock came round then five past: he checked his watch against the time on the kitchen clock. Ten past: he started to think no one was coming, after all the cottage wasn't the easiest place to find. Finally, at just after quarter past, there was a knock at the front door. A woman was standing there, mid to late twenties he guessed, with a sallow complexion and short mousy coloured hair brushed back off her face.

'I'm Mandy,' she said as she stepped inside then, after she took her coat off and put it over the back of a chair, she added 'It's forty for straight sex. Anything else is negotiable. The money first if you don't mind.'

Tim fetched out the wad of notes, peeled off two twenties and handed them to her.

'Is this where we're going?' she said casting her eyes round the room with its loose-covered sofas and stone inglenook fireplace. 'You've got it nice and cosy here....I didn't catch your name on the phone.'

'Tim,' said Tim.

There was a smell of stale cigarette smoke on her clothes and yellow nicotine stains on her fingers. A cold draught was coming from under the door.

'Look,' he said. 'I don't think I can go through with this. I'm sorry. Keep the money.'

She looked at him. 'We can sit down and talk if you like. You might feel different in ten minutes.'

Tim shook his head. 'I'm sorry,' he repeated.

'Have you done this before? Paid for it?'

'No. Never.'

'You're married?'

'Separated.'

'You're sure about the money?'

'Yes, keep it. I'm sorry for wasting your time.'

She picked up the notes. As she put her coat back on Tim caught another waft of stale cigarettes. He watched as she made her way down the front path but then for the first time he noticed there was a car parked in the lane with a man sitting inside.

'It's my minder,' she called back when she turned round by the gate and saw Tim still standing there.

The car started up and Tim craned his neck to get a better view of it. It was, he saw, a maroon Ford Escort with the number seven stencilled in a white circle on the side.

Back inside the cottage, he checked his watch. It was ten to three and just enough time to drive into town and take the video back. As he left he noticed the dark mass of clouds gathering in the sky to the north-west. He decided to go straight on at the crossroads and follow the narrow twisting lanes into town.

There were a few flurries of sleet as he pulled up outside the video shop. The man behind the counter was on the phone so he was able to hand over the cassette in its plain white box without getting drawn into conversation. Back on the street he walked up and down looking in shop windows feeling better for being out in the cold fresh air.

On the return journey to the cottage the sleet turned to snow and he began to regret going along the lanes again and not using the main road. The snow quickly became a blizzard making it difficult to see in front. Headlights on, windscreen wipers struggling, he was hoping the snow wouldn't settle and he'd find himself stuck in a drift in the middle of nowhere. On one steep part he felt the tyres slip but he kept going until he eventually came to the crossroads where the fury of the blizzard started to lessen. Just a few more yards, all downhill, and soon he'd be safely back home. He prepared to make the right turn onto the piece of spare land at the side of the cottage. As he did he chanced to look in the rear-view mirror. At first he couldn't make it out then he realised someone was standing back at the crossroads. A solitary figure dressed all in grey with a hood drawn over its face.

Tim got out of the car quickly. Who on earth would be out at the side of a lonely country crossroads in weather like this? He grabbed his thick winter coat from the back seat determined to find out. The blizzard had almost stopped, just a few flakes of snow still falling from the sky, but, when he looked up towards the crossroads, there was nobody there. He zipped up his coat and started to walk back to where he'd seen the mysterious figure. Over in the direction of the village the dark opaque mass of the snow storm was fast receding into the distance. When he reached the crossroads he searched the ground for footprints but the thin covering of snow was already starting to melt. In the end he gave up telling himself the figure he'd seen was probably just some rambler caught out in the snow or a farm worker making his way home.

★★★

Almost a week passed by before Tim saw Jen Mortimer again. The need to do some more shopping forced him into making a trip into town where he came across her walking along the High Street.

'Let me buy you coffee,' he said after they'd stood talking for a few minutes.

There was a small café overlooking the market place where they bought two espressos from the self-service counter and sat at a table by the window.

'So how's business?' said Tim taking off his scarf.

'Ticking along,' she replied taking a sip of coffee. 'Repairs and alterations continue to pay the bills but the big ambition is still to design and make my own range of clothes. I'll get there some day.'

'How long have you been going on your own?'

'Here? Since the autumn.'

'And before?'

'I was in London and other places.'

'Doing what?'

'Much the same kind of thing. Bits here and there. Occasional work for the theatres.'

'So what made you come to this part of world?'

'A lot of things happened,' she said turning her head to one side to look out of the window. 'It's a long story.'

Stallholders on the market poured hot drinks from their flasks. Red faces chapped by the wind, thick coats with turned up collars, pigeons strutting around picking at bits that had fallen on the floor.

'And how goes it with you?' she said turning back. 'Still settling in?'

'Slowly,' Tim answered. 'The pace of life takes a bit of getting used to.'

She finished her coffee and Tim offered to get her another.

'No thanks,' she said shaking her head. 'I must get going. Two deliveries to make before lunchtime.'

Back outside he watched her walk off across the market place struck once again by something about her that he couldn't quite put his finger on.

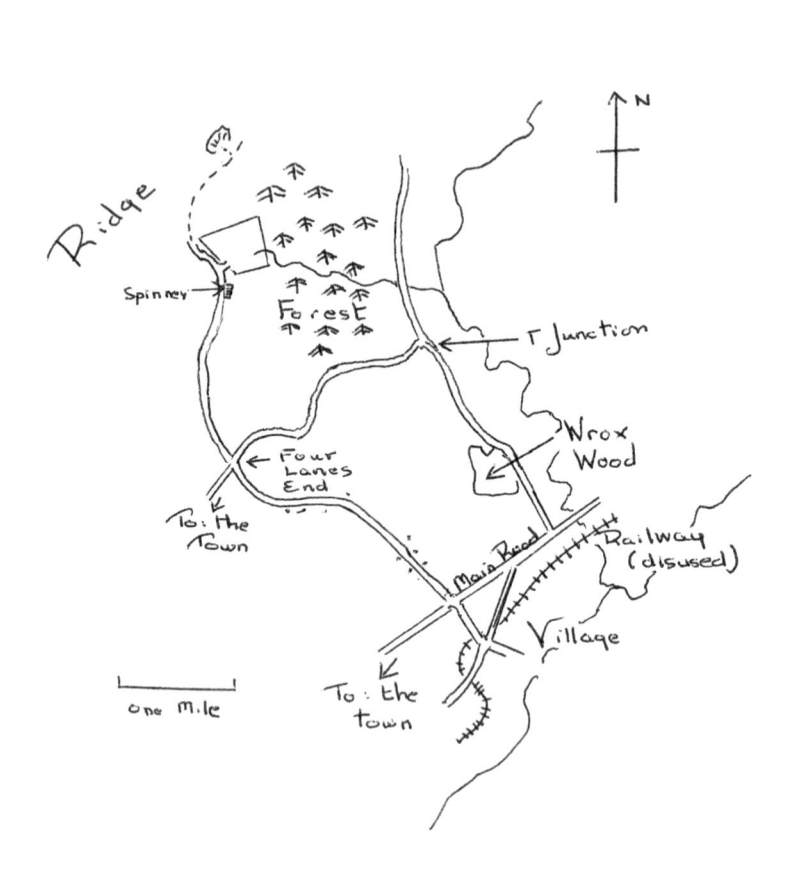

CHAPTER NINE

Larches

A FEW WEEKS LATER

'Hi.' It was Jo's voice on the other end of the line. Moon checked to make sure the office door was shut then went over to the window where the signal strength was better.

'Charlie, I had a call from Steph Holt last night. She'd been thinking and wanted to add some more to what she'd already told me about Leinthall Williams. Are you free to talk?'

'Yes, fire away.'

'Apparently he made his pile back in the seventies promoting rock groups. You know what I mean; they got the fame, he got the money and, along with the money he got the big houses, the big cars, a yacht he keeps somewhere down on the south coast and a taste for fancy living. Then, about ten years ago, he decided to ditch the boy bands and move into property development.'

'You mean doing up houses and selling them on?'

'No, I'm talking about the big league: buying up rust belt sites and turning them into out-of-town shopping malls, leisure complexes, that kind of thing.'

'He made an even bigger pile?'

'That's only half of it. After banking his first million he went in for a complete image makeover. Out went the black t-shirts and the pony tail, in came mixing with the toffs in his waxed coat and green wellies.'

'How does Steph know all this?'

'She kept Williams on her radar. She knows people who work in the music business and she started putting out feelers. Williams, it seems, has a reputation as a sexual predator going back years. Vicky Rodericks wasn't the first. Twelve and thirteen year olds round the back of concert halls. He prefers them young but Steph says he'll go after anything in a skirt.'

'Jo, there's nothing on criminal records to back what you're saying. Williams is a clean as a whistle as far as any previous form is concerned.'

'Come off it Charlie. You know as well as I do that most of these cases go unreported. Young girls like Vicky. Too frightened to say anything. Knowing if they do nobody will believe them.'

'Jo, don't get me wrong. If Steph Holt has got any evidence that could lead to a conviction she should take it straight to the police.'

'You're missing the point Charlie.'

'Am I? In which case please explain.'

'The reason Steph rang me. She was telling me to be careful. She thinks it's me who's interested in Williams because that's what I told her to shield you. She wanted me to know he's got a nasty temper which, coupled with his arrogant streak, could make him dangerous. Steph was worried I might get hurt.'

★★★

Thompson, Scott and Tamberlin were gathered in the small conference room. Moon muttered his apologies for being a few minutes late then turned to the first item on the agenda which was the line of enquiry Thompson was following up with GPs and hospitals in the area around the crime scene. The thinking was someone with gonorrhoea would have to go and get treatment.

'Nothing doing,' Thompson reported. 'No one had any record of a patient with a sexually transmitted disease named Mattox and the GP he's registered with in Hereford hasn't seen him for years.'

'He must have caught it off someone,' said Moon scribbling on a pad to get his ball-point to work.

'Yes Guv, I did try asking for a list of cases they'd treated in the last six months to see if it triggered anything we'd find interesting.'

'And?'

'I got lectured a few times about the protocols of accessing medical records. No one seemed too keen to act off their own bat. Two of the hospitals said they'd have to refer the request to higher management. So far I've heard nothing.'

Next on the list of subjects for discussion was the photograph of Mattox taken from his crime sheet which Scott and Tamberlin were going to try hawking round from door-to-door to see if it helped trigger anyone's memory.

'What happens if we draw another blank?' Tamberlin asked with a look on his face which told everyone around the table that he thought the whole exercise was a waste of time. 'Where we might have more joy is by releasing his picture to the press along with an appeal for anyone who's seen him recently to come forward.'

'Let's see first,' said Moon.

Thompson exchanged glances with Tamberlin. Both of them knew Moon would have to get clearance from Willoughby before involving the press: something they knew he wouldn't be keen to do because of all the fuss and performance involved.

★★★

The monthly senior management team meeting had been slotted in for mid-day with Willoughby in the chair as usual. The meeting started with a few words from Willoughby about being glad to be back followed by a general bollocking for all on the subject of being more vigilant when it came to signing off officers' expenses. Moon soon found himself drifting off, switching his attention to the rear of Millership's head which he could see from his seat in the back row. Willoughby droned on, pausing every so often to pour a glass of water from the decanter in front of him. Doctors' orders, Moon didn't doubt.

When the meeting ended Moon filed out with everyone else. Time to make himself scarce, a voice in his head told him. Time to pay another visit to the crime scene.

He left site at just after one-thirty, stopping off at the sandwich shop to pick up a baguette before settling back for the drive into the country. He slipped a compilation of field recordings from the forties and fifties into the CD player and, for the next hour, listened to the voices of convicts and drifters singing about their troubles. From time to time he checked behind but for most of the journey he had the road to himself.

He decided first of all to take a look at the village. He carried on past the turning to Wrox Wood until he came to a fork to the left which took him past fields where cows and sheep were grazing. It started to spot with rain and he thought about Scott and Tamberlin out there somewhere showing the picture of Mattox to the locals. It reminded Moon of the stern warning Willoughby had just issued about car sharing. He'd laid it on the line that officers should always travel together when going to the same destination.

He was in the village almost before he knew it. The church with no spire was at the centre, the telephone box outside a pub called The Red Lion. There was a village green of sorts with a kiddies' climbing frame in the middle. A few people about in spite of the rain: a young woman in a plastic rain hat pushing a pram; an old man standing outside the pub either going in or coming out.

At the far end of the village he came to where the road went over a humpback bridge. Just before the bridge there was a large open space on the right where he stopped. He reached over to the glove compartment where he'd put Thompson's OS map which he'd helped himself to earlier. A quick glance confirmed that this was the place where a country station had once stood but where there was nothing now except for a few mounds among the weeds and the rusty remains of an old gas lamp. The humpback bridge no longer spanned the railway tracks but looked down instead on a wilderness of dead willowherbs and thistle heads.

The last track of the CD finished and, apart from the noise of the engine ticking over and the occasional scrape of the windscreen wipers, it was all quiet. He spread the map out across the steering wheel and studied it more closely, fixing his eyes again on the places where conifer trees grew. He noticed what he noticed first time. Most were on higher ground a long way from the crime scene but there were a few exceptions and the time had come to check them out.

Pausing just long enough to finish the baguette, he slipped the car into first gear and, with the steering wheel on full lock, he turned round so he was facing in the direction he'd just come from. Back through the village, the woman with the pram had gone but the old boy was still hiver-hovering outside the pub.

He spent the next half hour driving round wet country lanes gazing at woodlands and plantations. No sign of any larch trees anywhere while he noticed daylight was slowly starting to slip away. He had one last place he wanted to check. He drove up a lane between smallholdings and orchards. A cottage here and there and, at one point, a more modern-looking bungalow where a black cat sat outside the front door. The lane was getting steeper until after a quarter of a mile he came to a crossroads where he stopped to check the map for the umpteenth time. He saw he needed to go right, another lane except this one was narrower. He passed a cottage with lights on inside and a trail of smoke coming out of the chimney. On he went, the lane so narrow now he hoped and prayed no one would come the other way. After less than a mile he pulled over by a farm gate, turned off the engine and got out into the rain.

There, exactly where the map said they would be, he saw the dark shapes of conifer trees silhouetted against the sky at the top of a steep rise. From this distance it was impossible to make out the species so, after making sure he'd left enough room in the lane for cars to get past, he changed into his wellingtons and his rainproof high vis jacket. Setting off up the slope he found it harder going than it looked and halfway up he came across a fence line half hidden in the bracken consisting of two strands of rusty barbed wire stapled onto stout wooden posts. He stepped over it, taking care not to catch his trousers. The trees were now in front of him: tall trunks with bark knotted like plaits in a rope and planted in rows. Larches. He stopped to get his breath back then turned round. He could see the car where he left it and, half a mile away, the headlights of traffic on the main road. Larches, and he knew down there somewhere in the gathering darkness lay Wrox Wood.

CHAPTER TEN

The Watcher

A FEW WEEKS EARLIER

Tim was in the kitchen when he saw Jen's van pull up on the front. It was just after eleven one Saturday morning. He'd been living at the cottage for nearly two weeks.

'I'm sorry to intrude,' she said as she came in. 'I wasn't even sure I'd come to the right place.'

Tim took in her appearance. She was wearing the same jumper and pair of jeans she wore the first time he'd seen her. The look on her face told him something was wrong.

'I feel such a nuisance,' she said when she'd finished explaining about water gushing out of a pipe at the side of the bungalow.

Tim picked up the box of tools he kept under the kitchen sink. Jen meanwhile reversed the van on the piece of spare land where he kept the car.

'When I took on the lease the agents gave me the number of a firm to ring if anything needed fixing,' she said as they drove back to the bungalow. 'I tried them earlier but all I got was a recorded message saying their office is closed until Monday. How silly can you get?'

When they reached the bungalow she drew up on the front.

'This way,' she said pointing to a path leading round the side. They came to where water was pouring out of an overflow and creating a flood on the paving slabs.

'Is it serious?' she asked.'

'I'll tell you when we find out where this is coming from,' Tim replied.

The problem turned out to be the float valve inside the toilet cistern in the bathroom. It was stuck.

'Probably because it's new,' said Tim freeing it with his finger. He flushed the toilet then waited for the cistern to fill again to satisfy himself the valve was working properly. He repeated this several times before putting the lid back on the cistern.

'All done,' he said.

She thanked him but Tim shook his head. 'All part of being a good neighbour,' he said. 'Besides it could be my turn next to come knocking on the door asking to borrow a cup of sugar. Or looking for someone handy with a needle and thread to sew a button back on my shirt.'

She smiled. 'I'll do us something to eat,' she said leading the way through to the kitchen where he'd been before.

Later they sat down at the kitchen table tucking into toasted cheese sandwiches.

'I appreciate I'm not doing much for my image as the totally capable modern woman,' she said. 'I'm not normally this helpless when I'm faced with having to deal with a crisis.'

'Did I hear you say you're renting this place?' Tim

asked casting his eyes around the shelves with the glass jars and cookery books.

'It was advertised as a refurbished post-war bungalow with a small studio workshop,' she replied. 'There's an option to buy in the lease but I'd rather see how the business is going before I start thinking about putting roots down. Till then, I'll keep an open mind.'

'You're happy living on your own?'

'I've got my cat for company,' she said dabbing a crumb from the corner of her mouth.

'What about the locals? Do you have much to do with them?'

Jen shook her head. 'I keep away from the village if that's what you mean. Villages are gossipy places where someone like me wouldn't fit in. I do all my shopping in town.'

She drove him back to the cottage. 'You must let me repay you in some way,' she said as she watched him get out. 'That's twice now you've come to my rescue. What about letting me buy you a dish of pasta one evening? There's a new place in town we could try.'

★★★

The next day was blustery with a wild wind from the west which had got up in the night. Tim's first job was to go out in the back garden to inspect a piece of guttering which had come down although, thankfully, he could see that all it needed was to fix it back into its bracket. The eaves of the cottage were low and he managed to reach the bracket by using a pair of steps. When he finished he spent a few minutes looking round the neglected beds where someone had once grown flowers and vegetables. The old greenhouse with some of the panes of glass still in their frames, the wheelbarrow tipped over on its side and, over in one corner, a cold water storage tank looking like it had been thrown out years ago. He came to the overgrown hawthorn hedge which marked the boundary to the plot of land. Beyond was the field he'd looked at many times: left fallow with the remains of last year's arable crop still in the ground.

Just at that moment something caught his eye. Over on the far side of the field he thought at first it was an old sack blown into the bushes by the wind. Then he realised. A figure in grey with a hood drawn over its face and his mind went racing back to the figure he'd seen standing at the crossroads in the snowstorm. He felt his pulse quicken. Someone watching him and, if so, who and why? The figure was still standing there little more than a hundred yards away. Feeling the urge to get to the bottom of this mystery, he looked round searching for a gap in the hedge he could squeeze through. He came to the old greenhouse and found a place where he reckoned, with a good push, he could force his way to the other side. He kept his eyes fixed on the figure. Still it stood there. Still with its face hidden. Still motionless.

Using his forearms to protect himself from getting too many scratches he shouldered his way into the hawthorns feeling the thorns and twigs catching at his sleeves. The edge of the field had been left to go back to nature and he stepped across it warily not knowing what lay hidden in the grass and weeds. He was still wearing the pair of old pumps he'd put on to go outside and mend the gutter and, because the soles were worn smooth, he found himself struggling more and more to keep his footing. Away from the shelter of the hedge he started to feel the blast of the wind cutting across the field. All the time he stayed focused on the figure which had remained so perfectly still it had started to go through his mind it might be an effigy someone had put there to scare off the crows. He was drawing closer, close enough to see the figure was dressed in what looked like a cloak but then suddenly it seemed to become aware of his presence. Its head came round and for a fleeting second Tim thought he caught sight of something white under the hood. He quickened his pace and then, one moment the figure was there, the next it vanished.

Cursing the wretched pumps which made it impossible for him to break into a run without slipping over, he trudged across the last few yards of the muddy field until he stood staring down at the spot where the figure had stood. The ground was trampled, he noticed as he searched round looking for clues. In front of him a dense coppice offering any number of possible hiding places. He waited to see if anyone broke cover but nothing happened and in the end he turned round and looked back towards the cottage nestling in its hollow on the far side of the field. Now for the first time he saw how from here the lie of the land offered a perfect vantage point for anybody wanting to observe his movements. Was he being fanciful? Or was someone who dressed up in a cloak and a hood keeping tabs on him for some reason?

The wind was getting up again catching the smoke from the chimney and twisting it into swirls. He stood there for a while lost in his thoughts then noticed a familiar figure coming towards him. It was Joe Darby walking along the edge of the field with Jack the fox terrier darting in and out of the long grass and looking like he was following a scent.

'Is anything wrong?' said Joe when he was close enough to see the expression on Tim's face. Joe was wearing the flat cap and belted overcoat he always wore.

Tim looked at him. 'Someone was there,' he said pointing to where he'd seen the strange figure.

'I didn't notice anyone,' said Joe. 'Did you see who it was?'

That's just it,' said Tim then explained the figure in grey always had a hood drawn over its face.

'You've seen it before?'

'Once,' said Tim. 'On the day it snowed. It was standing up by the crossroads.'

'Well there's a thing,' said Joe taking his cap off to scratch the top of his head in the way Tim had seen him do before. 'It sounds to me like you've seen The Watcher. It's been a while since he put in an appearance and there's a few in the village who say his time is due.'

'The Watcher?'

'What you believe is up to you,' said Joe leaning forward on his stick. 'But according to the story a gallows once stood at Four Lanes End where they hung people such as witches, murderers and highwaymen. Some say The Watcher is the hangman from back in those days who returns every so often to look for his next victim.'

'A ghost? You're asking me to believe that's what I've seen.'

'Like I said, what you believe is up to you but you won't be the first to see The Watcher and I dare say you won't be the last.'

Tim stood there slowly shaking his head from side to side.

Joe hadn't finished. 'There's something else I ought to tell you about The Watcher. Some people say he's a bad omen. Death is never far away when he puts in an appearance but I wouldn't lose too much sleep over it if I was you. Most of these village tales are nothing but nonsense.'

CHAPTER ELEVEN

The Last Chance Saloon

A FEW WEEKS LATER

Moon took one last look at the larches as he removed his wellingtons and put them back in the boot of the car. The light was almost gone but he could still make out the tall line of shapes at the top of the steep rise. His thoughts turned to Mattox in his shirtsleeves and his fancy trainers. Was this the way he came on that fateful day? Emerging from the forest, blinking as he came out into the light and seeing the descent down into the lane in front of him? Hesitating perhaps; as a stranger would in a strange place? Running away but running away from who and why?

A few spots of rain started to fall on the windscreen as he drove off with his headlights on full beam. After no more than a mile he came to a T junction where he turned right. Driving slowly, taking in every feature along the way, seeing a barn owl flit silently over the top of the hedge and coming finally to Wrox Wood where the crime scene tapes were still in place and a police van was drawn up on the verge but no sign of anyone sitting inside. He carried on until he reached the main road where he waited for a gap in the line of traffic before he pulled out.

★★★

'Can you spare me five minutes?' It was ten past ten the following morning. The voice on the phone was Willoughby's.

Stand by, Moon said to himself as he stopped off in the gents to straighten his tie. He glanced down at his shoes which still had a few scuff marks from his trip out into the country. He got rid these by rubbing his toe caps on the backs of his trousers, a feat he accomplished by holding on to the sink and balancing on one leg at a time. Up the flight of wooden stairs to the top corridor then the long walk to Willoughby's office at the far end. The silence only broken by the soft padding of his feet on the carpet tiles reminding him of the day when he'd been summoned here two years ago.

Pausing in front of Willoughby's door he took a deep breath before knocking on it three times.

'Come.'

Moon walked in to find Willoughby alone at his desk.

'Take a seat,' he said pointing to the vacant chair positioned in an acre of space facing him. It went through Moon's mind at this point to ask Willoughby if his throat was better but somehow he couldn't get the words out. Sucking up to authority had never been one of Charlie Moon's strong points. Willoughby spoke.

'Charlie, this is off the record. Just between the two of us, you understand?'

Moon said nothing. He waited for Willoughby to continue.

'I wanted to ask you about Detective Sergeant Thompson. Do the two of you still get along or has there been any friction recently?'

Moon looked at him. Thompson? This was a new one. Moon took his time answering knowing he could be heading into a trap.

'I'm not aware of anything,' he replied finally. 'As far as I'm concerned Detective Sergeant Thompson and I have a good working relationship.'

'Good. Excellent. So there are no concerns on your part that Detective Sergeant Thompson may be withholding information from you?'

'No sir. None.'

Willoughby picked up a paper knife and held it with the sharp end resting delicately against the tip of his middle finger.

'Charlie, I'll come to the point. I had a phone call from North Wales Police when you were out of the office yesterday. It seems Detective Sergeant Thompson had a conversation with one of their officers concerning a case involving a man named Williams. Did Detective Sergeant Thompson tell you about this conversation?'

'Yes sir. He did.'

'Ah, then perhaps you will be able to explain to me what this is about?'

'The Mattox enquiry sir. DS Thompson was running a check on licensed shotgun owners living in the area around the crime scene and Williams' name came up.'

'The murder weapon being a shotgun?'

'That's correct sir.'

'This man Williams is a suspect?'

'No sir.'

"Oh, so what was the justification for DS Thompson contacting North Wales Police? Presumably he had a good reason."

'Williams has a history sir. In 1997 he was charged with raping a young girl.'

'And DS Thompson felt it might have a bearing on your enquiries?'

'Yes sir. That's correct.'

'Did it?'

'Did it what sir?'

'Have a bearing on your enquiries?'

Willoughby was still holding the paper knife. Still with the point resting against his middle finger.

'It might suggest Williams has a tendency towards violence.'

'You're not overlooking the fact he was acquitted?'

'No sir. I'm not.'

'Have you arrived at a motive for the killing?'

'Not so far sir. Nothing's come to light yet to link Mattox to where his body was found.'

'Or to Williams?'

'No sir.'

'Are you aware that North Wales Police had to pay out a substantial sum of money to Williams when the case against him was dropped?'

'Yes sir, I heard something along those lines.'

'So it would be reasonable on their part, would it not,

to wonder what was going on when they heard we had taken an interest in him?'

'Yes sir, I can see that.'

'Yet it didn't occur to you that I needed to be brought into the picture? No alarm bells rang out in your head?'

'I'm sorry sir; I don't follow.'

'Don't you? In which case let me explain. I emailed you several times to get an update on the Mattox enquiry and, when you did eventually design to reply, you made no mention of Williams. Similarly you made no mention of Williams to DI Millership when he asked you to fill him in. Sometimes I don't get you Charlie. It's like you've got an aversion to communicating and, this time, it was me who was made to look a fool when I couldn't answer questions being put to me by one of my opposite numbers in another force.'

'I'm sorry sir.'

'So you should be. Time and time again I've had to have these conversations with you about keeping me informed but here we are again, back in the same old place. Moon who wants to run things his way. Moon who thinks he knows better than everybody else. Well, frankly Charlie, I'm sick and tired of it. I don't want to be looking over my shoulder all the time wondering what you might be getting up to. I want to be told what's going on. Do you understand?'

'Yes sir.'

'Right, so what's the latest with Williams? What do I tell North Wales Police when I ring them back? Is he aware DS Thompson has been making enquiries about him?'

'Not from anybody at our end sir.'

'Good. So this has gone no further than DS Thompson speaking to the officer in North Wales?'

'No sir.' Moon felt a dry patch on the roof of his mouth. There were the conversations he'd had with Jo Lyon. Now he'd be well and truly for the high jump if ever these came out. Willoughby was speaking again.

'Let's make this plain Charlie. I don't want to be put in embarrassing situations by you thinking you can go round making up your own rules. I let you off the hook two years ago but I'm starting to think I made a mistake. Perhaps you can't teach an old dog new tricks after all. We'll see but don't let it escape your attention that this is it. You've tested my tolerance to the limits. From here on you're drinking in the Last Chance Saloon. Got it?'

As he made his way back down the corridor Moon ran his finger round the inside of his collar consoling himself with the thought it could have been worse. As he reached the top of the wooden staircase he heard a door click behind him. He turned round just in time to see the grey suited figure of Millership making his way into Willoughby's office.

Seeing no sign of Thompson and the others and feeling the need for some space, Moon gathered up his overcoat and made his way to the car. He checked the time. It was just after eleven. Too early to think about lunch, he drove out to the piece of derelict land overlooking the railway lines where he slid a CD into the CD player and eased his seat back a couple of notches. His thoughts turned to Willoughby and Millership back at HQ with their heads together. He knew he'd played right into their hands and, the more he thought about it, the more he realised he only had himself to blame.

A freight train rumbled past hauled by a diesel engine daubed in graffiti and belching out a plume of thick black smoke. His eyes fell on the OS map still on the passenger seat where he'd left it the day before. He picked it up and spread it out across the steering wheel. Wrox Wood circled in Thompson's red marker pen, he saw again the features he'd already noticed many times: its slightly irregular shape, the little deciduous tree symbols, a red arrow Thompson had drawn pointing to the spot where Mattox's body was found then the lane running down one side where, if Moon's guess was right, the running man in shirtsleeves saw someone coming after him and took to the trees.

Still keeping his finger on the map Moon then traced the lane back to the T junction and, from there, to the left until he came to the place where he'd parked the car and climbed up the steep bank to get a closer look at the larch trees. Mattox with water marks on his chinos, Mattox who'd paddled through a pond or a stream at some stage of the flight that took him to Wrox Wood: Moon pored over the map looking at every little detail knowing, with Willoughby on the warpath, this was one case he needed to wrap up quickly. A few seconds later his eyes fell on something he hadn't noticed before.

CHAPTER TWELVE

The Feel of New Life in the Air

A FEW DAYS EARLIER

Tim picked Jen up at seven thirty as arranged. They drove into town and parked on the old cattle market. Jen wore a long black winter coat over a plain woollen dress and boots with low heels. Tim did his best to look smart wishing though he'd hung onto some of the suits he'd taken to the charity shop thinking he'd have no further use for them.

The restaurant was only a stone's throw from the car park. It was new yet small and cosy with candles on the tables and a blackboard menu on the wall. When they were seated Tim told her about the mysterious hooded figure he'd seen and the story of the hangman from years ago who came back to claim his next victim.

'Do you believe in the supernatural?' she said when he finished.

Tim shrugged. 'It's not something I've ever really thought about. Besides I'm sure most of these things have perfectly normal explanations. Nothing to do with spirits of the dead or anything else spooky.'

'What about this ghost?' she asked.

Tim laughed. 'I'd put my money on some local nutter who gets a kick out of standing in hedgerows. I'm certain no one in their right mind would act in such a strange way.'

As the evening went on and the mood became more relaxed, Jen talked about spending three years at art college when she left school and deciding while she was there she wanted more out of life than a husband, two kiddies and a three up three down on a new estate. She trained as a seamstress and learned the trade by moving from one fashion house to another. Tim listened noticing how the soft candlelight played delicately on the fine features of her face. There was a strength there but also a frailty.

'What about you?' she said abruptly as if wanting to move the subject of the conversation away from herself.

'There's not much to tell,' Tim replied. 'I only ever worked for one firm. Apprentice of the year at sixteen, youngest ever Section Leader at twenty three, Technical Manager at thirty two and now out on my ear at forty. I got the push just six months short of chalking up twenty five years' service. I never did get to pick up the gold watch.'

'You must have felt angry.'

'At first, yes, but I think I've managed to put the negative thoughts behind me. It took a long time but I've learned to move on and stop dwelling on the past.'

Being mid-week most of the tables in the restaurant were empty. In the end Jen and Tim were the only ones left.

'Don't forget this is my treat,' Jen insisted when the time came for paying the bill.

Tim went to protest but she stopped him.

'Okay but only on condition I pay next time,' he said thanking her.

They walked back to the car park. It was a mild balmy night with a fresh scent to everything. A reminder Spring was just round the corner and, with it, the feel of new life in the air.

It was just before eleven when he dropped her off at the bungalow.

'I've enjoyed this evening,' she said as she got out of the car.

'Me too,' said Tim.

He walked her across to the front door and waited while she looked in her bag for her keys. As he drove off he saw her stoop down to pick something up and, when she stood up again, he noticed she was holding the black cat in her arms.

★★★

After a good night's sleep, Tim breakfasted next morning on muesli, dried fruit and fresh orange juice. He felt good and the feeling persisted as he set off with his rucksack on his back and his thoughts on spending the day tramping around outdoors in the open air. It was still mild with a gentle breeze coming from the south. Everywhere birds were singing: blackbirds, robins, song thrushes and, in the hedgerows, he noticed new buds starting to shoot.

When he reached the crossroads, he paused to take in the view finding, as he did, his thoughts turning again to Jen and the unexpected direction events in his life seemed to be taking. He didn't stop long and set off up the narrow sunken lane with its pungent earthy smells and the steep banks on both sides where he imagined primroses would soon be blooming. He came to the field with the sheep and wondered how long it would be before he saw the first lambs. He kept his eyes fixed on the two narrow strips of tarmac stretching out as far as the next bend. He saw no one. He had the lane all to himself again.

He came to the two stone pillars and the place where he'd had the encounter with the dog. He approached cautiously remembering this time to stop and look round in the hedgerows for something he could defend himself with. He came across a stake of blackthorn which broke off easily and, as he inched forward, he kept his eyes peeled for any sudden movements in the bushes beyond the cattle grid. Once he was safely past he picked up his pace again but, just before he did, his eyes fell on a detail he'd missed before. A steel letter box had been bolted into the stonework of the left hand pillar. It made Tim smile to himself. The postman delivering the mail could do his job without having the seat of his trousers ripped out by the hound from hell.

Still with the blackthorn in his hand, he quickly covered the last few yards to where the hard surface of the lane ended. He was back tramping in the mud of the old cart road following it to where the steep path went off to the left which would take him to the top of the ridge. Climbing up and up he came to the open downland and places where rabbits had made burrows in the hillside. At the top he took in the view of the wide and misty dale beyond. He kept walking keeping to a path which followed the crest of the ridge. On both sides the landscape was spread out like a map and, to the west, he could see the dark outlines of distant hills. The sun came out and, high up in the sky above his head, a plane flew over, a tiny silver dot leaving behind two thin jet trails across a pale blue winter sky.

After walking for about twenty minutes he came to what he quickly realised was the rim of the old quarry where he paused to look down. Beneath him the sheer drop into the bottom where the milky still surface of the pool reflected the colour of the sky. Nothing moved and the strange feeling returned of intruding where he wasn't wanted.

Seeing no way forward he turned round and went back. There were a few more clouds in the sky but nothing to suggest the weather could change to rain. His spirits were still high as he retraced his steps. He felt on top of the world.

When he arrived back at the top of the steep path that would take him back down into the trees his thoughts turned to finding somewhere to sit down and eat his sandwiches. He chose a clump of tussocky grass which felt dry to the touch and slipped the rucksack off his shoulders. Soon he was tucking into the three rounds of cheese and onion on rye bread he'd prepared before he came out. As he sat there looking at the view his eyes picked out the twisting course of the lane heading back down the hill towards the crossroads. He took a sip from one of the bottles of spring water he'd taken out of his rucksack but, as he did, he caught sight of something. A car coming up the lane? He couldn't be sure. He put the bottle of water down and took out the binoculars which were still in his coat pocket but, even with their help, it was hard to see anything because the tall overgrown hedgerows stood in the way. He waited, keeping the binoculars fixed to his eyes.

Five seconds, ten seconds: if it was a car it was moving slowly but at last he had a clear view. Coming round a bend, a silver coloured Range Rover with a face behind the windscreen. He quickly lost sight of it again but then, as he panned the binoculars round, he saw he was straight in the line of sight of the two stone pillars. He waited again but nothing happened. Slowly he put two and two together. The Range Rover had stopped but why? Soon he had the answer. Down by the pillars a man appeared on foot wearing a green quilted body warmer over an open-necked shirt. He was standing there doing something but Tim couldn't see what it was until he realised. He was retrieving letters from the letter box and looking at them. Was this the same man who called Bob Preece a peasant and who everybody did their best to avoid? Tim had no idea but he carried on watching although, from this distance, he found it hard to pick out anything distinctive about the man's features. Finally the man walked off and, half a minute later, Tim saw the Range Rover as it rattled across the cattle grid.

But, just as Tim was on the point of putting the binoculars back in his pocket, something else caught his eye. On the opposite side of the lane to the two stone pillars was a place where the hedge grew so thick it had become a dense tangle of briars and brambles. Standing there with its back to Tim and just a few yards from where the man in the body warmer had stood to look at his letters was the grey hooded figure. Tim tried to adjust the binoculars to get a better view. At first the figure kept perfectly still, the hood drawn over its face, but then, after half a minute, it stepped away and vanished into the bushes. What struck Tim though as he watched it was the stealth with which it moved. Like a wild animal stalking its prey.

CHAPTER THIRTEEN

The Culvert

A FEW DAYS LATER

Moon hit the eject button of the CD player and pulled the lever of the car seat to bring it back into the upright position. His eyes were still glued to the map, still spread out on the steering wheel in front of him, where, a few seconds earlier, he had noticed something he hadn't seen before. A thin blue line marking the course of a stream cutting its way through the larch trees and difficult to make out among the jumble of spot heights and contour lines. A stream anybody doing a runner through the forest would have to cross over and there perhaps was the explanation for how Sean Mattox managed to get the bottoms of his trousers soaked.

★★★

The morning following the dressing down from Willoughby was grey and dreary with a fine drizzle in the air. Moon set off at shortly after ten and stopped at a garden centre for a cup of coffee where he sat at a table on his own.

Just before noon he pulled up in the narrow lane

at the foot of the steep bank in exactly the same place he'd left the car two days before. As he got out into the cold and damp he automatically looked up. The hillside was shrouded in low cloud which hung in the trees because there was hardly any wind. He changed into the wellingtons and high vis jacket again and set off up the slope where droplets of water and spider webs clung to everything. He came to the fence line and stepped over it exercising the same care as before to avoid snagging his trousers on the barbed wire. Reaching the top of the bank he turned round to look back at the view. This time, however, the visibility was so poor it was hard to make out anything. Even the noise of the traffic on the main road was muffled by the mist.

Pushing on into the dark depths of the forest he found himself in a still dripping world where there was nothing to be seen except for rows of trees going off into the distance. No landmarks, no paths to show him the way, he saw straight away how easy it would be to get lost and spend hours wandering around. Gradually his eyes grew more used to the dim light. Trees, trees and more trees going on and on and never ending but then suddenly and without warning, a flashback came to him. The dream he'd had of being in a forest just like this one and the feeling the trees were closing in on him. Then the cry that came from nowhere, except this time the cry was real, not something created in the imaginings of his sleeping mind. He stopped in his tracks. There it was again, coming from high up in the treetops, a cry piercing the stillness of the forest but then, as he stood there looking up for the explanation, it came to him. A kite or a buzzard, a big bird of prey, either circling over the forest canopy or perched somewhere on a high branch where he couldn't see it.

He set off again but he'd not been walking long before the ground in front started to fall away and he found himself looking down into a deep valley from where the sound of rushing water reached his ears.

Taking care not to slip on the loose layers of earth and larch needles he made his way down the steep descent taking it a step at a time. The last few yards were a scramble but finally he stood on the bank of a fast running forest stream which had etched a channel into the bedrock. He stopped and stared but, as he did, his heart sank. The stream was no more than a yard wide so all somebody wanting to get across would need to do was step over it.

Another theory gone tits up, Moon muttered to himself as he looked round noticing the cold air in the valley bottom and the pungent damp smells. A place where the sun never reached and where nothing grew apart from the giant trees. As he stood there he toyed briefly with making his way back to the car and writing the day off. Scott and Tamberlin wouldn't be too far away hawking their picture of Mattox round door-to-door and, as it was getting close to lunch time, he could arrange to meet up with them for a sandwich and a pint. Something was telling him though not to give up just yet. This hidden place deep in the depths of the forest could still have secrets to reveal.

For no reason other than following one of his hunches he decided to make his way upstream. He picked his way round fallen branches and exposed tree roots. In places twigs and other pieces of debris had made small weirs in the stream over which the flow of water spilled. He heard the buzzard again but this time the cry came from further off.

Climbing all the time he came in the end to what appeared to be the head of the valley where, through the trees, he saw something up ahead which puzzled him at first until he saw what it was. A stone wall, a full ten feet high, cutting straight across his path, looking big enough and old enough to have once been part of some ancient fortification. The ground in front of the wall fell away adding even more to its height and ruling out any possibility of scaling it from this side without the help of a rope or a ladder. But just as Moon was wondering what to do next his eyes were drawn to where a culvert, a low-arched tunnel, had been built under the wall to allow the stream to pass beneath it. With gathering interest he went across to take a closer look. The culvert was small but Moon figured at a push it could take a man providing he crouched down low enough. Seeking to put his theory to the test Moon lowered his foot gingerly into the stream but withdrew it quickly when he realised the water would come over the top of his wellingtons.

Interesting, Moon said to himself, as he bent down as far as he could go to try and get a look inside the culvert and, as he did he felt a waft of cold air on his face. He could see light at the other end and, halfway along, stubs of ironwork projecting from the roof where it looked like a row of bars had once hung presumably with the aim of stopping intruders getting through. Was this the way Sean Mattox came? Up to his knees in water getting away from somebody coming after him?

Realising he would have to come back equipped with a pair of waders if he wanted to investigate further, Moon stepped away from the bank of the stream and looked at the wall again. All around him the eerie stillness was starting to feel oppressive. He remembered the OS map in his pocket and fetched it out. Unfolding it, he quickly picked out the stream with its steep sided valley and where he'd followed it as it cut its course further and further back into the hillside. He saw the thin black line he now knew to be the wall and then his eyes fell on something else. On the other side of the wall what looked like a country estate with a big house sitting in the middle.

***

Back at the car Moon took his wellingtons off and, out of curiosity, inspected the soles. They were thick in mud, a sticky mixture of loam and larch needles which would be difficult to wash off without the help of a high-pressure hose. As he stood by the car door he looked back at the trees only to find the mist had come down so it was impossible to see them.

He prepared to drive off but, as he did, the phone rang. At first he couldn't make out anything but then he realised it was Scott with his voice breaking up badly.

'Guv, we need to talk,' Scott was saying through the background of crackles and echoes. 'Something unexpected has just turned up.'

CHAPTER FOURTEEN

A Knock on the Door

A FEW DAYS EARLIER

Tim left it a week before he rang Jen on the number she'd scribbled down on a piece of paper. Whether it was his wishful thinking or not, she seemed pleased to hear his voice and accepted straight away when, after insisting again it was his turn to pay, he suggested a return visit to the restaurant where they'd dined the first time.

He picked her up the following evening at just after seven. On the journey they talked about this and that but it wasn't until they were sitting in the restaurant that Jen brought up the subject of the hooded figure and whether he'd seen it again. In between studying the menu and ordering food, he told her about the strange scene he'd witnessed through his binoculars on the day he sat up on the ridge.

'What did you make of it?' she asked using a cocktail stick to pick up an olive from the dish which had been put in front of them.

Tim shrugged his shoulders. 'Hard to say,' he replied. 'Except what I've thought all along. Some head case with nothing better to do than stand in the bushes watching people.'

'Not a ghost?'

'Not a ghost.'

'What about the man in the Range Rover? Have you seen him before?'

Tim shook his head. 'I'd hazard a guess he's the owner of the property at the top of the lane with the warning on the gate to keep out. Not a friendly type by all accounts.'

The place was starting to fill up. A party arrived and took a table at the far end which looked like it had been laid up specially for them.

'There's something I ought to tell you,' Tim said when they were halfway through their first course. 'I'm married. I'm sorry I've been meaning to tell you. I know I should have mentioned it before.'

'Before what?'

'Before anything. Before asking you out for dinner this evening.'

She smiled. 'You think it would have made a difference? I would have said no because of something in my little book of rules about not going out with married men?'

'Tonight is tonight but you still have a choice. You can walk away if you want to. I would be the first to understand.'

'What do you want?'

'I think you know the answer.'

She smiled again and this time he noticed the same trace of sadness in her face he'd noticed before.

'I didn't plan on meeting you,' he said. 'Things at

home went from bad to worse after I lost my job. In the end I felt I couldn't take any more but, rather than sit down with her and try to sort it out, I took the coward's way out. First I found a place to live then, once Christmas was out of the way, I put my belongings in the boot of the car one morning when she was out and drove off.'

'She has no idea where you are?'

'I didn't leave a note if that's what you mean.'

'Is that how you intend to leave it?'

'I don't know.'

'She must be worrying.'

'Yes I realise.'

'Are there children?

'Two: Simon's the eldest; he's nineteen. Sonia is fifteen and still at school.'

'Do you think about them?'

'Sometimes.'

The party at the far end were celebrating an occasion. Two bottles of champagne appeared and toasts were called.

Tim waited for the noise levels to die down before he spoke again. 'That's not all,' he said. 'My real name is Tim Giffard. I'm not proud of what I've done.'

'There's no need for explanations,' she said. 'Life is life. It isn't always a bed of roses.'

'Are you happy for us to go on meeting like this?'

'We're both grown-ups,' she said.' Don't build your dreams on me, that's all. What I do today may not be what I want to do tomorrow and, when the time comes to move on, I want to be free to go without anybody pulling at my heartstrings. No, let me finish,' she said when he went to speak. 'I don't want you getting hurt. I don't want me feeling I've let you down. Do you understand?'

A few more people drifted in. The candle on the table flickered in the draught from the door casting shifting patterns of light and shade across her face.

Tim spoke. 'I take the days as they come,' he said. 'It's a lesson I learned a long time ago. Expect nothing. Accept what's given. Don't be disappointed when it's taken away. I'm not looking for a wife substitute if that's what you think. Will I change my mind when the novelty of living on my own wears off? Will I start to get fed up with cooking my own meals and making my own bed? The honest answer is I don't know. I don't think I will but that could be just the way I see things now. Happiness is brief. Treasure it while it lasts.'

***

For the next few days Tim busied himself with jobs around the cottage but then, one afternoon, there was a loud knock on the front door. When he opened it he saw two young men standing on the path.

'Good afternoon,' said the man who was closest. 'My name is Detective Constable Scott and this is Detective Constable Tamberlin. We're making a few enquiries in the area and we've got some questions we'd like to ask. It shouldn't take too long. Is it all right if we come in?'

CHAPTER FIFTEEN

The Runaway

The small conference room had been taken over at short notice by three grim looking types from the Internal Audit Team leaving Moon equally grim faced and with no choice other than to hold the meeting in his own office. Thompson was last to arrive. It was ten o'clock on the dot and, with a squeeze and thanks to extra chair purloined unofficially from somewhere along the corridor, they all managed to sit down.

'Over to you Scotty,' Moon began. 'I've heard all this before but Dave here needs to be brought up to speed.'

Scott shuffled his papers and cleared his throat. 'This was yesterday afternoon,' he said. 'Tambo and I went back to this cottage where we've been before but never found anybody in. This time a character answered the door who gave his name as Stafford. When we showed him the picture of Mattox he said the same as everybody else: he'd never seen him before and the name meant nothing to him. When we asked him if he'd seen any strange faces lately or anything unusual going on he said he'd only been living in the area since the start of January. He'd never heard of Wrox Wood and, when we showed him where it was on the map, he said he'd driven that way a few times but, other than that, he didn't know it.'

'In short nothing suspicious up to this point?' Moon interjected.

'No Guv; except Tambo and me both had the feeling he wasn't telling us everything.'

'So who thought to check out the registration plate of his vehicle?'

'That was Tambo,' said Scott. 'He made a mental note of it as we left.'

'Yes,' said Tamberlin taking up the story. 'His car was parked on a piece of spare land at the side of where he lives. A Renault 21 first registered in 1992 belonging to someone named Giffard with an address in Wolverhampton.'

'Not Stafford?'

'No Giffard.'

'We made a few enquiries when we got back,' said Scott taking over again. 'Then it all came out. The Giffard in question went missing from home just after Christmas and, according to what police in Wolverhampton told us, his wife still has no idea where he is. He lost his job at the back end of last year and, by all accounts, he took it badly. At first the police thought he might have gone off somewhere and topped himself but now it looks like there was more friction going on at home than the wife originally let on. What clinched it for the police was when they found he'd packed all his personal effects into a suitcase the day before he disappeared plus it came to light later he'd withdrawn six thousand pounds in cash from a joint savings account.'

'Not what anybody would be doing before throwing themselves in the canal.'

'No Guv.'

Thompson stopped doodling on his pad. 'Scotty what are we talking about here in terms of distance between where Stafford stroke Giffard lives and the crime scene?'

'Two miles at the most,' Scott replied. 'The cottage stands on its own in a quiet country lane with next to no traffic.'

Thompson again. 'If Stafford is Giffard does he have any form?'

Scott shook his head. 'No, Wolverhampton had him checked out but we ran his details through Criminal Records again just to be sure. Clean as a whistle. Wolverhampton also spoke to his old firm and even they couldn't fault him. A spotless record stretching back almost twenty five years so it seems.'

Thompson pulled a face. 'And this is the villain we're hoping to hang a murder charge on?'

'What about firearms?' said Moon. 'Has anybody done any checking yet to see if this man is licensed to own a shotgun?'

'That was the next job on the list,' said Tamberlin. 'We're also getting some photographs sent over so we can make a more positive identification. The description Wolverhampton gave us over the phone seems to fit but we'll be happier when we've clapped our eyes on him.'

'Anything else?'

'No Guv.'

'Okay,' said Moon 'Let's leave it there for now. With an unsolved murder just down the road somebody posing as somebody else calls for further investigation but let's not get too carried away. There could be nothing more to this than a runaway husband doing his best to cover his tracks. Dave....'

'Yes Guv.'

'Can you stick around for five minutes? There's another matter I want to talk to you about.'

Scott and Tamberlin filed out. Moon closed the door after them then went over to where his coat hung from a peg on the wall and took out the OS map which was still in one of the pockets.

'This place,' said Moon after he'd spread the map out on the desk. 'I want to know who lives here.' He was pointing to the area of parkland circled by the stone wall he'd stood in front of the day before.

Thompson turned the map round to get a better look. Moon continued. 'Don't talk to anyone unless you have to and, if you do, keep my name out of it.'

Thompson nodded. He'd spent enough time under Moon's tutelage to know not to ask questions when the instructions his boss gave seemed strange. He also knew life at Team Penda meant his chief had to spend a lot of his time walking a difficult political tightrope.

Thompson picked up the map as he went out. When he'd gone Moon's eyes drifted across to the one-eyed monster which he'd switched on earlier only to find another day had gone by with no emails from Willoughby. He looked out of the window, parting the slats of the blinds with the tips of his fingers. There outside were Willoughby's and Millership's cars parked next to one another with their paintwork gleaming in the morning sun.

Ten minutes later Thompson was back.

'I thought so, he said. 'When I put together the list of people who own shotguns I plotted each one using a grid reference. The place in its own grounds surrounded on two sides by trees is called Edge House. Guess who it belongs to?'

CHAPTER SIXTEEN

Keeping Bad Company

The morning after the two detectives came knocking on the door Tim decided to go for a walk hoping the fresh air would do him good. He'd spent the night tossing and turning and, to add to the burden of what was going through his mind, he'd tried ringing Jen several times only to find the line went straight onto the answer machine.

As he set off up the lane he wondered about turning left at the crossroads and going to see if she was in. Something warned him though that, on a day she would be working, it might not be such a good idea. He decided therefore to go right and up the narrow sunken lane.

There had been a sharp frost in the night and a thick layer of rime covered everything. A morning mist made it impossible to see any further than a few yards in front while the sound of his footsteps on the cracked and pitted surface of the lane seemed to follow him as he passed between the steep earthen banks and overhanging hedgerows.

When he reached the gate he could hear the sheep in the field but couldn't see them. As he climbed further up the hill past familiar waymarks he got the impression the mist was thinning out. His thoughts had meanwhile gone back to the two detectives and the news they brought of a dead body being discovered not far away. They'd showed him a photograph of a man, a face which meant nothing to him. Then the questions. Had he seen anything unusual in the last few weeks? Had he noticed any strangers? He answered no to everything. He didn't tell them about the strange procession of cars he'd seen on the night he hid behind the holly bush or the mysterious hooded figure. He wanted the detectives to go away feeling they'd done their jobs. He wanted the name Tim Stafford crossed off their checklist. He didn't want them stumbling on the truth about who he was and what he was doing shacked up on his own in this out of the way place. He knew at the same time he was treading on thin ice and it was this knowledge that had kept him awake half the night.

Past the spinney of trees shrouded in mist; past the stone pillars and the cattle grid; past the place where he'd seen the hooded figure from his lookout on the ridge; past where the course of the wall changed direction and disappeared into the trees: he came to the old cart road where he paused to slip the rucksack off his shoulder and take out a small bottle of water. The water tasted good: cold, sweet and refreshing but, as he stood there taking sips, his eyes fell on something. In the mud at his feet, looking like they'd been freshly made, were a set of tyre marks. Somebody lost? Somebody who'd driven up this way then reversed back when they found the lane went no further? Yet the tyre marks went on.

Putting the half-empty bottle of water back in his rucksack he set off again following the twin lines of marks in the mud which were easy enough to pick out as they swerved in and out of the ruts and potholes. Into the scattered woodland and the ashes and the whitebeams to where the path up to the ridge went off to the left. The tyre marks kept going and, as he walked along with his eyes fixed firmly to the ground, he remembered the rainy day and the last time he'd come this way. Several times he thought the sun might break through but it didn't. On he went noticing after a while a strange smell. At first it came and went then it grew stronger. An acrid burning smell, oddly out a place in the cold fresh morning air.

He came to where the cart road opened out into the flat open space and there, looming out of the mist in front of him, was the entrance to the old quarry and the haunted looking derelict building with its broken windows. He paused, taking in again the sense of brooding which hung about this place. It was then he saw the burnt-out car. Abandoned over by the edge of the opaque milky coloured pool with its registration plates missing and still smouldering. He made his way across to take a closer look but, as he did, he quickly realised this wasn't just any old burnt-out wreck but a Ford Escort where, beneath the blistering paintwork, he could see traces of red and the faint outline of a white circle on the driver's door.

'I'm glad you came along.'

Tim turned sharply. It was Joe Darby standing by a boulder which had come down off one of the rock faces.

'I'd say this hasn't long been done,' Joe said pushing his cap back off his forehead as he came across. 'Somebody reckoning on not many people coming this way. A gang of these joy riders. Kids with nothing better to do than go round stealing cars then, when they've had their fun, setting fire to them. Or somebody else perhaps. Somebody with different reasons for wanting to get rid of something they didn't want left on their hands.'

Tim stared blankly at him. His thoughts were on the man in the baseball cap, Mandy's minder. The man who, if he was the same man, he'd seen sitting behind the wheel of the Escort on the night it trailed behind the procession of 4x4s.

Joe was standing in front of him leaning forward on his stick. 'I know you know who it belongs to,' he said. 'I saw it outside your place one afternoon. No I don't want to poke my nose in where it's not wanted but, if I was you I'd think carefully. There's always a right and a wrong way of doing things but sometimes it's hard to know which one's which.'

'Have you reported this to the police?' Tim asked.

'Not yet but now you're here I'll leave it to you to decide what's best.'

Jack appeared.

'He's got the scent of vixens,' Joe said with a smile. 'It's their time of year to be out and about.'

They went back along the old cart road together: Jack sometimes tagging along behind them, sometimes disappearing into the trees. Joe spoke.

'Talking about the police I expect they've been to see you about the dead body that's turned up. What they won't have told you is that it was Jack who found it. You have to say some strange things have started happening round here.'

They came to the stone pillars followed by the spinney of trees.

'I'm going this way,' said Joe pointing with his stick. 'There's an old footpath which goes across the fields and it's easier on your feet than walking on the lanes.'

Tim watched him go. There was a gap in the hedge which was barely noticeable and the broken remains of a stile.

'I know it's none of my business,' said Joe as he climbed over the stile. 'All the same, if I was you, I'd be more careful about some of the company I keep.'

CHAPTER SEVENTEEN

A Man of Principle

Moon arranged to see Jo in a city centre bar, one of the places they'd used for clandestine meetings in the past. It was up a side street and away from the hustle bustle of evening rush hour. As he left HQ Moon took all the usual precautions to make sure nobody was following him. He doubled back a few times, took detours through brightly lit industrial estates and kept a careful eye in the mirror. When he was satisfied he pulled on to a multi-storey car park then completed the journey on foot. It was just after six when he arrived.

'Sorry I'm late,' he said to Jo who was sitting in a corner by herself with two glasses and a bottle of wine on the table in front of her.

'Drinks are on me,' she said as he took his overcoat off and hung it over the back of a chair. 'Now tell me what all this is about. You sounded tense on the phone.'

Moon looked round to see no one was in listening distance before he started to speak. First he told her about the meeting with Willoughby.

'What do you think he's up to?' Jo said topping up his glass.

'Apart from satisfying the need to bring me down a

peg or two I'd say he was genuinely narked he'd been caught with his pants down. He needed to get his control back by asserting his authority over me.'

'Wouldn't you say that shows signs of insecurity?'

Moon laughed. 'I'd put it more bluntly. When something comes along which has the potential to blow up in his face, he shits himself. His whole act is geared to putting on the right appearance. Getting out there catching criminals takes second place.'

'But there's more to why you wanted to see me than getting a few grumbles off your chest?'

'Too true,' said Moon. He then filled her in on what he'd discovered on his walk through the forest. He told her about Edge House, the country pile surrounded by a ten foot wall which, he now knew, was home to none other than Leinthall Williams.

'Let me get this straight,' she said when he finished. 'You think these trees and the tunnel you found could point the finger at Williams being at the bottom of all this?'

'I'm saying it could all be a red herring but the only hard pieces of forensic evidence we've got to go on are the larch needles embedded in the bottom of Mattox's trainers and the water marks on his trousers. The tunnel connects to Williams' estate which could just be a coincidence of course.'

'So where does your investigation need to go next?'

'Under normal circumstances? We'd be having words with Williams to find out what his movements were in the time frame we think the murder was committed. Depending on what he had to say for himself we might need to get a search warrant to go over his property and at the same time check out any guns he currently owns.'

'So what's stopping you?'

Moon smiled. 'I'd have to get clearance from Willoughby first. If I didn't and I went in off my own bat without telling him he'd have my head in a vice.'

'You're not suggesting Willoughby would put the brakes on a murder enquiry?'

'No,' said Moon. 'But with what happened in North Wales he'd see the potential for Williams and his legal team claiming police harassment. North Wales didn't manage to pin a conviction on him back in 1997 so in 2001 they get their pals down in the Midlands to do the job for them.'

'Charlie, I'm not sure I'm following this. If Williams is guilty of murdering this man Mattox then what the police in North Wales and Birmingham are up to behind the scenes is irrelevant. If he shot somebody and, if the evidence is there, he goes to prison. Okay I can see what you're saying about Williams' London barristers putting up smokescreens but, at the end of the day, that's all they'll be. Smokescreens.'

'What I'm saying Jo is I know Willoughby and I know he won't want yours truly handling an investigation where the conduct of serious crimes officers could become an issue. He spends his time watching his back and he'll see straight away his position could come under attack. No, he'd have me whipped off the case straight away and hand it over to someone who could be relied on to follow instructions.'

'Wait a minute, Charlie, four years ago a poor innocent

girl was systematically raped and now someone has been murdered. Surely this is about more than which one of you brings the culprit to book. You may not like the idea of Millership or somebody like him muscling in on your territory but surely it comes secondary to getting Williams put behind bars.'

'Jo, the point you're missing is that, if Millership is put in charge of the investigation, he'll play by the rules. He'll look for cast iron evidence before he starts putting the screws on Williams. A few larch trees and a tunnel under a wall won't cut it. He'll want to find something more, something which links Williams to Mattox, and he'll start from the premise why should a wealthy businessman who owns a large country estate want to mix with a low life whose main claim to fame appears to be fixing up his mates with knocked-off tellies?'

'You're saying the investigation would be kicked into the long grass? Williams could walk off scot-free again?'

Moon remained silent.

'What's become of the Charlie Moon I once knew?' Jo continued. 'Leaving aside Mattox, look at Williams' track record. Look at what he did to Vicky Rodericks. Look at what he's done to countless others. Think of your own daughters.'

'You're suggesting I should bend the rules?'

'Why not? That's what you've always done in the past when you've thought the issues were more important than paying lip service to the stupidity. You've followed your own conscience and, yes, I know it's sometimes got you into hot water but you've always stuck by what's right. You've shown the world you're a man of principle. You may not always play by the book but your record speaks for itself. You get scum like Williams put away.'

'There's something else to tell you,' Moon said. 'A character living under a false identity has come to light living in the vicinity of the crime scene. His real name is Giffard and all we know about him so far is he ran off from his wife six weeks ago.'

'You're treating this man as a suspect?'

'We only came across him yesterday so the answer at the moment is no.'

'But you're saying Williams may not be the murderer after all?'

'I'm not saying anything until we have more information.'

★★★

Next morning Moon started the day by holding a catch-up meeting with Thompson, Scott and Tamberlin. They were squeezed into Moon's office again, sitting shoulder to shoulder like sardines in a can. First item on the agenda was confirmation from Scott and Tamberlin that the absentee husband from Wolverhampton had never applied for or been issued with a licence for a shotgun.

'We could look into it further,' Tamberlin offered. 'He might have acquaintances with access to guns.'

'We'll come back to it if we have to,' said Moon. 'I'm conscious we've spent a lot of time chasing up blind alleys and, until we have more evidence this character is the man we're after, I'd rather hold off spending effort and resources going into the detail of his background.'

Next, Scott produced the set of photographs of Giffard which had been sent across from Wolverhampton.

'It's him all right,' said Scott passing the photographs over to Moon who hadn't seen them before. 'Tambo and me both said straight away you wouldn't mistake him in a million years.'

'It's not like he made any effort to grow a beard or dye his hair,' said Tamberlin. 'What you see there is exactly the way he looks now.'

Moon thumbed through the pictures studying each one in turn. They were not the standard mugshots of criminals he was used to seeing but family photographs looking like they'd been taken in the back garden or, in some cases, on holiday. They showed a man, no longer young, making an effort to smile. Some were with children, a boy and a girl, and, in one, he was standing next to a woman.

'That's his wife,' said Scott. 'Not hard to see why he left her.'

'Guv?' This came from Tamberlin. 'What happens if we're right and this is Giffard? Are we under any obligation to tell his wife where he's living?'

'Pass,' said Moon. 'Domestics are outside my field. She'll need to be told he's not dead but, where it goes from there, I haven't a clue.' He turned to Thompson. 'Dave, anything to add?'

'No, apart from asking Scotty and Tambo more about how Giffard came across when they interviewed him?'

'Nervy,' said Tamberlin. 'Definitely uncomfortable.'

'What, like he wasn't used to fending off questions from policemen or was there more to it?'

'How do you mean Sarge?'

'Was he covering something up?'

'Like what?'

'Something which might point to an involvement with Mattox for example.'

'You think we should get back in there and give him another grilling?'

'Perhaps that would be best left to me,' Moon interjected.

Scott and Tamberlin looked at him. 'Sorry Guv but I don't see where you're coming from,' said Scott. 'Tambo and me are both quite capable of coming on strong to Giffard if that's what you want.'

'I don't doubt it for one minute,' said Moon resting his elbows on the desk. 'But what I'm really thinking here is we may have to cut a deal with this character. He tells us everything he knows in exchange for us not blowing the whistle on him.'

'Guv, with respect, I don't see how that's going to work.' Tamberlin chipped in. 'Wolverhampton know we've located someone who could be Giffard and they're waiting for us to come back to them with confirmation one way or the other.'

'We'll face that one if we have to,' said Moon. 'What's more important now is we catch whoever killed Mattox. Helping Mrs Giffard go after her husband with a rolling pin fades into insignificance at the side of apprehending a murderer. Trust me, I know what I'm doing and, if there's any fall-out from this, it'll come my way not yours.'

CHAPTER EIGHTEEN

One Good Turn

Moon checked his emails again before he left although he'd already checked them several times that morning. There was still nothing from Willoughby suggesting that, for the time being at least, the Team Penda Commander's attention was turned elsewhere.

He stopped off at the sandwich shop to buy a baguette giving him the opportunity as he stood by the car to look round to see if anybody had followed him. The street was normally busy but a lull in the traffic allowed him to check the vehicles that came by one by one until he was satisfied nobody was cruising round the block waiting for him to pull out.

The drive out into the country passed by uneventfully. The sky was dull and overcast but it stayed dry. He slipped on a CD and let his thoughts drift off randomly. He ate the baguette as he drove along not noticing he was dropping crumbs on his trousers. He decided to steer clear of the crime scene and instead he drove up the lane which left the main road near the village and took a winding route past orchards and smallholdings. He'd been this way before on the day he discovered the larch trees. He remembered the bungalow where he'd seen the cat sitting outside but today the place looked quiet and shut up. He came to the crossroads where he paused as he had done the first time except, instead of turning right, the direction in which Giffard's cottage lay, he went straight on. He'd checked the map before he set out so he knew, if he kept going, he'd come sooner or later to the place where Williams lived.

The lane he drove up was a tight fit for the car but he managed to get through without scraping the sides. He steered round cracks and potholes and came to where the lane opened out. He expected to see farms and settlements but there was nothing except empty scenery. The lane went on, climbing higher and higher, until he came to what he was looking for. The entrance to an estate with two big stone pillars, one of which had a warning sign on it to tell would-be intruders to keep out. Edge House? There was nothing to say it was or it wasn't but Moon's eyes had already noticed the wall going off in both directions which left him it no doubt it was a continuation of the same wall he'd viewed from the other side of the estate after his walk through the forest. He checked the wall and the pillars for any evidence of CCTV. Finally satisfied his scouting expedition hadn't been caught on camera, he used the red shale drive to reverse into before heading back down the hill.

When he came to the crossroads again Moon realised he was close enough to see the chimney pots of Giffard's cottage. He checked the time. It was just after two and, with the hope he'd catch Giffard in, he coasted slowly down the last few yards to the front gate where there was a space on the verge wide enough for cars to pull in.

The first thing he noticed was the Renault 21 parked on a piece of spare land at the side of the cottage exactly as Tamberlin described. The front garden had a neglected look consistent with it being somewhere Giffard had rented in the short term while he got his feet on the ground. There was a heavy cast-iron knocker on the door which made Moon smile. In his long held opinion there was nothing better than a loud knock on the door to send shivers down the spines of anybody inside who might be harbouring guilty feelings.

'Good afternoon sir,' Moon said flashing his ID at the man who answered. 'I'm Detective Inspector Moon, Serious Crimes Team, West Midlands Police. You've already spoken to Detective Constable Scott and Detective Constable Tamberlin but I need a few more words with you. Inside if you don't mind.'

The man stepped aside and, as Moon went past, he made a guess he was about six feet tall while his face was without any doubt the face of the missing man from Wolverhampton. Dark hair going grey at the sides, slender build, fresh complexion, he was wearing a thick woollen jumper, black jeans and carpet slippers on his feet.

'A cup of tea would be welcome sir,' said Moon casting his eyes round. 'It's a long drive from Birmingham and I haven't had time to stop on the way.'

'Yes, of course,' said the man and Moon noticed the nervousness in his voice.

'Just a little milk and no sugar," said Moon as he continued to look round.

The man disappeared and soon Moon heard the clatter of crockery and the sound of a kettle boiling. The room he was in had a low oak-beamed ceiling while the central feature was an inglenook fire place where logs burned in an old-fashioned grate. There were two large sofas fitted with loose covers, a TV in the corner and a heavy oak dining table by the window with six matching chairs.

'Thank you sir,' said Moon when the man came back in carrying a tray with cups and saucers and a tea pot on it.

'Can we clear up one point that's been troubling us?' Moon began as he watched the man put the tray down on a small table in front of one of the sofas. 'You gave your name to the two officers who came to see to you and, when they checked it out, they found it to be false.'

The man was pouring the tea into the tea cups and Moon watched closely for signs of his hands shaking.

'Can I remind you sir that giving false information to police officers is an extremely serious matter?' Moon took the tea cup from him and sat down at the dining table helping himself to a coaster from the stack on the window sill. The man sat down opposite him. 'We're talking about a murder investigation here. A man has been shot, his body found in a wood not far away. In the circumstances I'm sure you'll agree that we have to treat anybody who is trying to conceal their identity as suspicious.'

The man said nothing. He sat staring vacantly in the direction of the fire place.

'The tea's very nice if I may say so sir.'

'It's nothing special,' said the man still gazing into space.

'Shall we go back to the beginning and make a fresh start?' said Moon. 'We know your real name is Giffard. You're on the missing persons list which is probably no surprise for you to learn. The police have been looking for you since just after Christmas.'

The man put his head in his hands. 'I've been a fool,' he said.

'Most people who're being honest with themselves realise they've been fools at some point in their lives,' Moon said. 'You left your wife. You won't be the first and you won't be the last.'

'I had nothing to do with your murder, I swear it. I came here to start a new life. The photograph your two officers showed me, the man's name, meant nothing to me.'

'Perhaps it would have been best if you'd told the officers the truth. If you had you wouldn't be sitting where you are now.'

'You don't think I did it?'

'That depends on how we get on today,' said Moon. 'I'm the senior officer in charge of this investigation so where we go from here depends mainly on me.'

'I've never been in trouble with the police in my life.'

'I don't doubt it sir.'

'I'm happy to tell you everything. Where do you want me to start?'

'With the murder victim please. You said you didn't know him.'

'No'

'He originates from Hereford. Do you have any connections with that city?'

'I've visited it a few times.'

'The last occasion being when?'

'Six or seven years ago. I took the children when they

were younger. I thought it would be interesting for them to look round the cathedral.'

'Your work, the people you socialise with, is there anything which links you with Hereford?'

'Nothing comes to mind.'

'What was your occupation?'

'I was a Technical Manager for a precision engineering company until last year when I was made redundant.'

'You never had any reason to visit Hereford in your professional capacity?'

'I occasionally went out to see customers.'

'But never to Hereford?'

'No'

'Let's move on to why you chose to come and live in this part of the world. I appreciate your reasons for not picking a place where it would be easy to find you but why here?'

'I came across the cottage by accident. Soon after I was made redundant I came out this way for a drive in the country. Why? To see if I could unclutter my head from all the negative thoughts going through it. Every time I came to a little lane I went up it. As often as not it turned out to be a dead end but then I saw this place with a 'To Let' sign outside.'

'You made enquiries about renting it?'

'Not straight away. I made a note of the letting agent's phone number. I contacted them in December with the idea of renting from the start of the New Year.'

'Which is what you did?'

'Yes.'

'I take it the letting agent would be able to confirm everything you've just told me?'

'I can't see any reason why they wouldn't.'

'And what you told the Detective Constables about moving in here in January is correct?'

'Yes. Is the date significant?'

'It means you were living here at the time we believe the murder was committed. You in your rented cottage living under a false name and, as the crow flies, no more than a mile and a half away from where somebody met a sticky end. Perhaps you can understand now why we need to clear up whether you had any involvement or not.'

The man said nothing.

'We'll turn to the crime scene,' Moon continued. 'An area of woodland the officers showed you on a map. You told them you'd only ever driven past it.'

'Yes.'

'You don't get about much on foot?'

'On the contrary I do a lot of walking.'

'But not past the place we're talking about?'

'No.'

'Still you must see a lot on your walks? People? Strange faces? Unusual goings on? People acting suspiciously? I'd think carefully before you answer. This is your one big chance to set the record straight. Tell me what you know about what goes on round here. Everything you've heard. Everything you've seen. Let me be the judge of what's important and what isn't.'

'Everything?'

'That's what I said. Don't miss anything out because it could have a big bearing on your future. Any more leaving out important facts wouldn't go down well for you.'

'Where do you want me to start?'

'Anywhere you like. People you've seen who don't belong round here may not be a bad place.'

'There's an odd character who turns up every now and then. Someone who stands in the hedges and watches what's going on.'

'Description?'

'I'm sorry I can't help you there. You see the character I'm talking about always wears a hood over their face.'

'You mean like a teenager in a hoodie?'

'No, more like someone dressed as a monk from medieval times. A grey hood and a long grey cloak. The whole outfit covers them from head to foot.'

'Have you any idea who this person is?'

'You're going to laugh at this. People say I've seen a ghost. An apparition who haunts the lanes round here.'

'You've seen it where?'

'Once on the far side of the field at the back, once up at the crossroads, once by the entrance to the big estate up the hill.'

'You mean Edge House?'

'I don't know the name of the place.'

'Have you reported these sightings to the police?'

'No. Never. If I did I had a feeling they'd want to take me off in a strait jacket.'

'Do you believe in ghosts?'

'In terms of figures in white sheets who go round rattling chains, no.'

'Shall we move on? Is there anything else unusual you've seen since you've been in residence here? Again think carefully.'

The man hesitated. 'What kind of assurance can you

give me that what I say will be treated in the strictest confidence?'

Moon looked at him. 'Without knowing what it is I can't say. Some information you provide may go on to form part of the evidence we have to present in court. In other areas we may be able to exercise a little discretion. Can you give me a clue what's troubling you?'

'I've met somebody here,' the man said with his cheeks turning red. 'There are some things I wouldn't want reaching her ears.'

'Your love life doesn't interest me Mr Giffard. I'm here to get to the bottom of a murder and find out if you've had any involvement in it. So far you've told me about a figure dressed in grey who looks like somebody from the Middle Ages and who may or may not be a ghost. So, in terms of establishing you're innocence, it would be fair to say we haven't made much progress. Regarding whatever it is you want kept under wraps, I am one of the dying breed of law enforcement officers who takes a broader view of life. Am I guessing correctly you've had your fingers in more than one pot of honey since you moved to the country?'

The man reacted angrily. 'I'm not a philanderer if that's what you think.'

Moon smiled. 'You tell me then Mr Giffard. What exactly have you been up to apart from taking long walks? And, while you're gathering your thoughts, another cup of tea wouldn't go amiss.'

While the man was out in the kitchen Moon stood up to stretch his legs. From the window, he could see the roof of his car parked out in the lane.

'I'll leave the tea to brew a little longer,' said the man as he came back into the room carrying the tray.

'You've chosen a nice place to live,' said Moon. 'It must be quite a change from Wolverhampton. Anyway let's go back to where we were, shall we? You were just on the point of telling me something delicate.'

The man's face flushed again. 'I did something I shouldn't have done. It was a big mistake.'

'We've all made a few mistakes,' said Moon allowing the man time to compose himself.

'I came across this woman's business card. I think you would describe her as a call girl.'

'Go on.'

'I phoned her up. God knows why. I think it was a mix of everything going round in my head.'

'You had sex with this woman?'

'No, I bottled out. I paid her for her time and she left. Afterwards I felt deeply ashamed of myself.'

He poured the tea and brought it across to the dining table where Moon had already taken his seat again.

'Was the woman local?'

'As far as I know. She had a local accent if that's anything to go off.'

'Mr Giffard I appreciate you telling me this but, unless I'm missing something, it doesn't appear to have a bearing on our enquiries.'

'There's more. As the woman left I noticed a car parked where yours is parked now. A red Ford Escort, quite unmistakable because somebody had painted a big number seven on the side. A man was sitting in it. I'm guessing her boyfriend or somebody she'd paid to give her a lift. It was the car that caught my attention though because I'd seen it before.' He then told the story of how one night he'd stood up at the crossroads and watched the Escort drive by on the tail of three 4x4s.

'Where were these vehicles going?'

'Up the lane which doesn't go anywhere except to the place you've just mentioned.'

'Edge House?'

'Yes: I've walked by it many times.'

'Who was driving the Escort?'

'A man wearing a baseball cap pulled down over his eyes. It was dark. I didn't get a good look at his face. It could have been the same man I saw driving the car the second time.'

'When the call girl paid you a visit?'

'Yes.'

'But you couldn't be certain?'

'I only noticed he was wearing a baseball cap. Both times.'

'When you saw the car the first time, was the driver on his own or did he have anybody with him?'

'There was somebody sitting in the passenger seat. I took it to be a woman.'

'The call girl?'

'I couldn't say. She was on the other side of the car from where I was standing.'

'Does the call girl have a name?'

'I only knew her as Mandy. I've still got her card.'

He went over to a small chest of drawers which also served as a telephone table.

'Here,' he said handing the card to Moon who

inspected it. Moon had seen many such cards before, most of them stuck to the insides of public telephone boxes.

'Back to the car,' he said. 'Have you seen it since?'

The man nodded his head slowly. 'Yesterday,' he said. 'I went for a walk and came across it abandoned in an old quarry. Somebody had set fire to it.'

'You're certain it's the same car?'

'You can still make out where the number was painted on the side.'

'Where is this quarry?'

'Go up the lane past the big house. Keep going and you come to it. It's not the sort of place anybody would find in a hurry.'

'Can you take me there?'

Twenty minutes later Moon in his wellingtons and high vis jacket was tramping along with Giffard at his side. They'd left Moon's car back where the lane past Williams' place came to an end and turned into a track. Moon checked his watch. It was half past three giving them two hours of daylight. Giffard hardly spoke a word apart from pointing out the tyre marks in the mud. They were passing through a wilderness of stunted trees, following the tyre marks to where they led eventually to the entrance to an old quarry. Moon had already picked up the smell of burning before he caught sight of the smouldering wreck resting on its wheel arches over by the side of a pool. He noticed how the registration plates had been removed so, whoever set fire to the car, had thought to put a screwdriver in their pocket. More telling was no second set of tyre marks made by a get-away car. Somebody had torched the car then walked away on foot with a set of number plates tucked under their arm. He noticed too the remains of the white circle painted on the driver's door exactly as Giffard described.

As they walked back along the track, Moon pointed to the wall to Williams' property which he could see over in the trees.

'How do you get on with your neighbour?' he asked.

'I've never spoken to him,' Giffard replied. 'I may have seen him in the distance once but never face-to-face.'

'Do you know anything about him? Anything which would help me piece together what this is all about?'

'I know people don't like him. I know there's a vicious dog running loose in the grounds of his house but, apart from that, I can't add to what I've already told you.'

'You can't shed any more light on what we saw back there at the quarry?'

'No, I'm sorry.'

Back at the cottage Moon stood with his back to the fire warming his hands.

'What happens next?' said Giffard.

'We'll need to do some checking,' said Moon. 'We need to be happy you're telling the truth this time.'

'How long will this take?'

'Till you know you're off the hook? It's hard to say but we'll do our best to get back to you as quickly as we can.'

'What about the matter of confidentiality we discussed?'

'What about it?'

'I need to know what I've told you won't become public knowledge.'

Moon looked at him. 'Shall we talk frankly Mr

Giffard? You want my help. You want your little dalliance with Mandy kept quiet so how would you feel about doing something for me?'

Giffard blinked.

Moon continued. 'The man who lives at Edge House is named Williams. I have a special interest in him and I want to find out more about what he does and who he mixes with without going through official channels.'

'I'm sorry, I don't understand.'

'I want you to keep an eye on him. Tell me if you see anything funny going on. See who visits him and what they get up to.'

'You want me to spy on him?'

'Spy isn't a word I'd choose. Helping the cause of justice is more the way I'd see it.'

'Is this to do with the murder of the man from Hereford?'

'It might be. It might not.'

'You want me to feed back reports?'

'Only to me you understand.' Moon pulled out a card with his contact details on it.

'What if I say no?'

'Think carefully before you do. Think about your new lady friend. Think about one good turn always calling for another.'

On the journey back Moon passed the time listening to music but, just as he was getting into a relaxed frame of mind, a chilling thought struck him. It was his wedding anniversary and the date had slipped his memory completely.

CHAPTER NINETEEN

Mandy's Story

Another domestic upset was averted thanks to the out-of-town shopping centre Moon passed on his way home. He bought a card, a large bunch of flowers and a bottle of champagne. He wrote the card in the car using the courtesy light to see what he was doing. A close shave, he told himself as he drove the last few miles. Ending up in the doghouse again had been narrowly avoided, at least until the next time.

It was eleven next morning when he managed to catch up with Jo. She'd been covering a case involving girls from Eastern Europe who'd been trafficked to work in a massage parlour on the edge of the city centre. Explaining she was pressed for time they agreed to meet for coffee at a place just round the corner from the law courts. At first Moon was apprehensive about the venue because the area would be crawling with police officers and people to do with the courts who would recognise him immediately. On the other hand nobody would find it unusual for him to be seen so close to the halls of justice. He decided to risk it.

Over two large Americanos Moon filled Jo in quickly on the events of the previous day.

'Any conclusions?' she asked.

'I'm not sure,' Moon replied.

'This man you've found hiding away from his wife, do you think you can count on what he told you?'

'The stuff about the ghost made me wonder but, on the whole, I'd say he was being straight with me.'

'All the same I don't see how it moves us forward very far. Williams mixes with dodgy people. Williams hangs out with hookers. Given what we know about him already, neither of these things could be described as surprising.'

'What are you doing tomorrow?'

'The court's not sitting so the plan is to have a long overdue day off. Why do you ask?'

'How do you fancy a drive out into the country?'

'With you!'

'I didn't know you found my company so unappealing.'

'There's a catch. I know you Charlie Moon and I know nine times out of ten you've got an ulterior motive up your sleeve.'

'I thought we were both on the same side.'

'What's that supposed to mean?'

'We both want Williams banged up.'

'Yes but you're the policeman not me.'

'I want to interview the call girl. I don't want to do it on my own.'

'Fine, get Sergeant Thompson to go with you. Unlike me he's a paid public servant.'

'I'll buy you lunch.'

'Come clean Charlie. You've got some reason for asking me. What's going on in that labyrinthine brain of yours?'

'Just one of my little hunches.'

'Don't bother to explain. You think this Mandy or whatever she's called will clam up if two big burly policemen come knocking on the door in their size twelve boots. You only want me there to provide the gentle womanly touch.'

'If that was the case I could call on the services of any of a number of perfectly capable female officers.'

'So why don't you?'

'Back to my hunch. Something inside tells me to keep people from the Team out of it until we've heard what Mandy's got to say. If I'm right she could prove to be the link with Williams and, as we know Williams is dynamite. The worst case scenario is everything finding its way back to Willoughby's ears before we're ready.'

***

Moon picked Jo up from her apartment at nine the next morning having taken the precaution of booking himself off on a day's leave. She was waiting, standing outside the two-storey apartment block in the leafy part of the city where she lived.

'I take it we won't be tramping through forests or paddling up drains,' she said pointing to the smart pair of patent leather boots she was wearing. She squeezed into the passenger seat doing her best to make room in the footwell where the plastic box containing Moon's precious collection of CDs took up most of the space.

They drove through the morning traffic taking numerous short cuts known to Moon thanks to all the years he'd spent dodging round bottle-necks in pursuit of his duties. They stopped at the garden centre where Moon paid for coffee and croissants. Jo looked round. The place was obviously a popular stopping-off point for retired couples with time on their hands. Mr and Mrs, they sat at the rustic wrought-iron tables eating their mid-morning brunches with little to say to one another apart from whether to splash out on another latte or ask where the draught was coming from.

'So what's the programme for today?' Jo asked using a paper napkin to wipe the crumbs off her fingers. 'Where have you arranged to meet this woman of the night?'

'We'll need to locate her first,' said Moon through a mouthful of croissant.

'You mean you haven't set anything up?'

'Is that a problem?'

'No, except you didn't warn me this was going to be a kerb-crawling expedition.'

'We've got this,' said Moon bringing out the card he'd taken from Giffard and passing it over to her. 'The phone number you see has been disconnected so we'll have to do some asking round. Taxi drivers and pub landlords are usually good at knowing where these girls hang out.'

'What's this?' said Jo turning the card over and pointing to where somebody had hand-written an address on the back.

'Ah,' said Moon taking the card off her again.

Jo spent the rest of the journey going through Moon's box of CDs and picking out ones which interested her. When they went past Moon pointed out the little lane which went to the wood where Mattox's body was found.

'Up there is where I discovered the larches,' he said

indicating where dark bands of forest covered the side of the dale they were driving along. 'Giffard's cottage is over to the left and Williams lives near the top of the hill.'

'Where are we going now?' said Jo.

'That address you found is in the town a bit further on. It's only a few miles. We should be there in ten minutes.'

When they arrived they found it was market day and Moon had difficulty in locating somewhere to park. Eventually – and after driving round for ten minutes – he came across a space in a side street from where they set out on foot. Once or twice Moon asked passers-by for directions. The quaint town centre with its old Norman church and its little courtyards and alley-ways was soon behind them and they were heading down a hill into an area which looked like it had seen better days. Moon cast his eyes round checking street numbers. They came to a small parade of shops with flats over the top.

'This is it,' said Moon indicating where a gap in the line of buildings led round to the back of the shops and a yard where wheelie bins where kept. A flight of wooden steps took them up on to an open balcony and a row of doors. Washing lines were strung out and Jo and Moon made their way past them to the flat at the end.

After two presses on the doorbell a woman with lank hair answered who Moon took to be in her thirties but she could have been younger. She was wearing a pink faded top and a pair of jeans.

'Is this you?' Moon said holding up the card.

The woman looked from Moon to the card and back to Moon again.

'I'm not in business any more,' she said and made to close the door.

'My name's Detective Inspector Moon,' he said swiftly putting his foot against the door jamb. 'I'm with the Serious Crimes section of West Midlands Police. This lady is Ms Lyon. We would like to speak to you please.'

'Police?' she said. 'What would the police want with me. I've done nothing.'

'I think it would be best if we came in,' Moon said. 'Hopefully we won't take up too much of your time.'

As they entered the flat Moon wrinkled his nose in disgust at the thick smell of cigarette smoke. The woman led them through to a small sitting room where there was a television in the corner with the sound turned down and a laundry drier standing in front of the electric fire with items of children's clothing draped on it.

Moon spoke. 'We're here to ask you about somebody we think you know named Sean Mattox, originally from Hereford or so we understand.'

'I haven't seen Sean in weeks,' the woman said. 'It's no use asking me anything about him because I don't know where he is.'

'I'm afraid to tell you he's dead,' said Moon. 'Shot at close range by somebody with a shotgun. His body was found in a wood by which time he'd already been dead for a few days.'

The woman felt for the arm of the imitation leather sofa which, apart from the television, was the only item of furniture in the room.

'I take it you know him,' said Moon. 'Was he one of your clients?'

The woman shook her head. 'He lived here with me,' she said sitting down on the sofa and putting her head in her hands. 'I've known him two or three years but he moved in coming up to Christmas. Paid his share of the rent, ran me round in his car 'cos I can't drive. Somebody shot him? I can't believe I'm hearing this.'

'There'll be an inquest in due course,' said Moon. 'I'll make sure you're notified of everything.'

'You'll want to ask me questions I expect.'

'I'd like to know when you last saw him.'

'I'm not much good at remembering dates.'

'Did you have an argument?'

'No, it was nothing like that. He went out on business and told me he'd be back in a couple of hours.'

'He didn't return?'

The woman didn't reply. Instead she just sat there staring into space.

Moon again. 'Did he say where he was going? Who he was going to see?'

'Him up at the big house,' she said. 'I told Sean not to have anything more to do with him but he wouldn't listen.'

'Can you give me the name of the person you're talking about?'

The woman shook her head. 'Sean knew him, not me.'

'You say Sean had business with him.'

'Sean's business has nothing to do with me.'

Jo came across. She'd been standing by the window which looked out over the front of the flat down on to the busy street beneath.

'You have children?' she said to the woman.

'A little girl,' she replied. 'My mother has her during the day. What I do makes it difficult.'

'The man who lives at the big house.' Jo spoke in a quiet, calm voice. 'If we're talking about the same man he's named Williams and he's got a history going back years of interfering with little girls. Those he really fancies he forces to have sex with him. Not just once but over and over again until he's satisfied himself. No, I'm not with the police but I and others like me want him locked up. Help us please.'

The woman stared at her. 'I warned Sean about being greedy,' she said. 'I told him fortunes only come at a price.'

'Perhaps it would be best if we started at the beginning.'

The woman nodded. 'What did you say this man's name is?'

'Williams. Leinthall Williams.'

The woman nodded again. 'I don't know if anybody's told you,' she said. 'Sean was one for going to the races which was where he met him and after they got talking in a pub. According to Sean he got all the rounds in and, when Sean started dropping hints he could get his hands on anything anybody cared to mention, the man said about a party he was throwing for some of his pals. What he wanted was a lap dancer but, on top of lap dancing, he wanted someone who would treat his pals to whatever they wanted. Sex with those who fancied it; blow jobs if that's what they preferred. He fetched out a big wad of money and Sean's eyes started popping.'

'Sean asked you if you'd do it?'

'He said there was a thousand quid in it for each of us.

In these parts it would take a lot of johns to earn that kind of money.'

'You agreed?'

'Sean was given a date not long after Christmas. We met up with these toffs outside a pub in town then Sean and me followed them in their big cars back to this place out in the country.'

'You say Sean got greedy? What was that about?'

'A few weeks before any of this happened, Sean got his hands on a load of camcorders which had fallen off the back of a lorry. He kept one for himself and, though I didn't know why till afterwards, he took it with him on the night of the party. The toffs were pretty pissed before they got there. It turned out they'd been out shooting in the afternoon then spent two or three hours in the pub knocking back whiskies.'

'Did everything go to plan?'

'As it turned out half the toffs were incapable of doing anything by the time we got round to the fun and games. Sean though was busy filming everything.'

'What did you think?'

'At first? I thought his idea was to see if any of the toffs would be interested in buying a film of themselves screwing or having their dicks sucked. When we got back though Sean came out with what he'd really been thinking. He reckoned these people were worth millions, big nobs who worked in the City, politicians, people who stood to lose a lot if what they'd been up to in private reached the wrong ears. He thought by putting the squeeze on them he could get them to pool together and pay him off.'

'He was going to blackmail them?'

'Sean worked out how much it would take for me and him to live out the rest of our lives in comfort. He had his heart set on buying a place in Spain. He said he'd done the sums, found out where to invest the money and what we'd need so neither of us would have to work again. He said what he was talking about would be peanuts to the kind of people who were in the room that night.'

'Did you believe him?'

'Not for one minute,' said the woman.

'Was this why Sean went to see Williams? To put the squeeze on him?'

'Somebody Sean knew put what he'd filmed on a video tape. Sean took it with him.'

'On the day he disappeared?'

'Yes.'

'When he didn't come back, what did you think?'

'Bad thoughts,' she said. 'Now you've told me Sean's dead I feel ashamed of myself.'

'You thought Williams gave Sean some money? You thought he had second thoughts about sharing it with you?'

'I didn't know he'd been shot, that was for sure.'

Moon took over. 'When Sean went to see Williams, did he go in his car?'

'Has it been found somewhere?'

'A red Ford Escort with a number painted on the side?'

'I don't know anything about cars. The number was Sean's idea. He thought it looked cool.'

'A car answering the same description has been discovered in an old quarry. Somebody dumped it there and set fire to it.'

'I don't know how Sean came by the car. I know it

wasn't taxed or insured. The tax disc was a beer bottle label. Sean thought it funny nobody ever noticed it.'

'I'm sorry about the next question,' said Moon. 'The pathologist who examined Sean's body reported that he had recently contracted a sexually transmitted disease. Do you know how that happened?'

'He caught it off me,' the woman said. 'He was going to the hospital to get treated but he hadn't got round to it.'

The woman gave her full name as Amanda Fownes. Moon warned her not to talk to anybody.

'We'll have some more questions in due course,' he said.

'This man Williams, do you think he killed Sean?'

'Our investigations are still ongoing Miss Fownes.'

'I warned Sean about getting on the wrong side of people with money. They always end up the winners.'

Back in the town centre Moon took Jo into The King's Arms for lunch.

'Have you been here before?' she asked as they sat down at a table in the dining room.

'Never in my life,' said Moon casting his eyes round at the other diners. Four middle-aged women were over in one corner looking like they were the committee of the local Townswomen's Guild. A young couple came in dressed in a way which suggested they were professional people on a lunch break from one of the nearby offices.

Jo chose a dish of locally caught poached salmon which came with helpings of new potatoes and fresh winter vegetables. Moon said he would have the same and together they chose a bottle of Sauvignon Blanc from the small wine list.

'Penny for your thoughts,' said Jo as they waited for their food to arrive. 'We know Sean went to see Williams but what do you think happened?'

'It's anybody's guess but I'd say at first Williams had difficulty in believing his ears when someone like Mattox turned up on the doorstep demanding money. Shocked, threatened, never thinking for one moment a lowlife like Sean would have the nerve to pull such a trick. How did he react? Again it's anybody's guess but, knowing what we do about Williams, I'd say it wouldn't be long before the red mist started to rise. Mattox, for his part, was probably banking on Williams crumbling so he wasn't prepared when things started to turn nasty.'

'You think Sean ran off?'

'That's my theory. Whether Williams pulled a gun on him by this point is a matter for conjecture.'

'I still don't understand why he made off on foot. Presumably he'd left his car nearby so why didn't he just get in it and drive away?'

'With Williams hot on his heels he may not have had the choice. Bear in mind Williams may have already taken a few pot shots at him.'

'Your guess is Sean discovered the culvert when he was trying to get away?'

'I'm saying there are still a few pieces missing out of the jigsaw but I'd put my bet on Sean making a dash for it in what he thought was the direction of the village. Why? There's a public telephone in the middle of the village where he could have rung for a taxi or phoned one of his mates to come and pick him up. What he didn't reckon on though was finding a ten foot wall standing in his way.

A bigger bloke may have been able to climb over the wall but, from what I saw of Sean's body in the mortuary, he only looked to be in the region of five foot eight or nine. Plus straddling the top of a wall wouldn't be the best place to be with somebody standing down below aiming a shotgun at you.'

'Do you think he knew about the culvert?'

'He may have done but, taking into account he hadn't been living in the area long, I'd say it was unlikely.'

'So how did he find it?'

'A stroke of luck or perhaps he came across the stream and took it in his head to follow it.'

'How far is it from where Williams lives to the place where Sean's body was found?'

'About two miles. Sean would have had to find his way through the forest first then, after that, I'm guessing he came out on one of the little lanes which criss-cross the area.'

'Do you think Williams chased after him?'

'Perhaps we'll never know but, if I had to hazard a guess, I'd say Williams drove round in his car basing his assumptions on Sean making for the village. As he approached Wrox Wood he spotted him up in front then, when Sean ran off into the trees, Williams got out of his car and went after him on foot. Why was Sean only wearing shirt-sleeves? I'd say either that was the way he was dressed when he went knocking on Williams' door or he jettisoned his coat at some point because it impeded his running. For all we know it could still be out there lying among the trees waiting for a search team to come across it.'

'So what happened to his car? How did it end up in the quarry?'

' I'd say Williams took it there.'

'After he shot Sean?'

'Not straight away. I'd say it was left sitting outside his house for a while or hidden up somewhere on his estate. He moved it when he heard Sean's body had been found. Why the quarry? Either he thought it wouldn't be discovered for a long time or setting fire to it would make it look like Mattox did it himself.'

'How do you know he didn't?'

'The car was still smouldering. Sean's been dead for weeks.'

'So is this where you go to Willoughby and say you want clearance to talk to Williams?'

'Possibly.'

'Any reason why you shouldn't?'

'Only the fear I've had all along he'll react by taking me off the case and giving it to somebody like Millership.'

'With a motive like blackmail I don't see how anybody, not even Millership, could stand in the way of doing what's right.'

'Don't you?'

'Don't just sit there being cryptic Charlie. Explain to me. What's bugging you?'

'Everything would hang on the say-so of a woman of low character: a prostitute who has probably got a list of convictions as long as your arm.'

'You're saying they'll think she made it all up?'

'I'm saying the likes of Millership and Willoughby would see straight away her evidence wouldn't count for much. Don't forget Williams would have the backing of his highly-influential friends standing up in court saying the police were trying to stitch him up.'

'Charlie, you're starting to make this sound like we'd need a signed confession from Williams before anybody did anything.'

'It's the way it is these days, Jo. I don't like it either.'

'What about this man Giffard?'

'What about him?'

'He saw Mattox and Mandy on the night of Williams' orgy. He could corroborate at least part of Mandy's story.'

'He saw a car answering the description of Mattox's car. It was dark. He was standing behind a bush.'

'But there's nothing wrong with his character.'

'It depends how you view somebody who's walked out on his wife and kids. Don't forget too he was on the phone to Mandy the minute he thought he was safe from his wife getting to hear about it.'

Later Moon dropped Jo back at her apartment just as the streetlights were starting to come on.

'Are you telling me everything today has been a waste of time?' she said searching in the bottom of her bag for her keys.

'Will Williams be getting away with it again?' Moon said drumming his thumbs on the steering wheel. 'Will he still be out there wrecking the lives of more innocents like Vicky Rodericks?'

'Well?'

'There's a last piece to all this, Jo.'

'Not another of your hunches Charlie?'

Moon smiled. 'It could be. Let's just wait and see.'

CHAPTER TWENTY

Justice By Other Means

It was starting to get dark as Tim backed the car off the piece of spare land at the side of the cottage. He wore his walking boots and the thick winter coat which still had the binoculars in one of the pockets. He drove up to the crossroads where he turned right, finding he had to drop into bottom gear to take the sharp corner. Passing between the steep banks and the overhanging hedgerows he came to the farm gate and the view across the fields. A heavy stillness hung in the air which he could feel even from where he was sitting inside the car. He carried on driving, staying in low gear, climbing the hill and passing the spinney where he saw the large grey shape of a roosting bird up in the trees. He came to the stone pillars then on to where the lane ended. Over to his left a thicket of hawthorns where there was just enough room to leave the car where it wouldn't be seen. He closed the door, a soft click, and then locked it putting the key away safely in one of his zip-up pockets.

There was silence all around, no birds, not a breath of wind in the air, and he went over again in his head what he was doing here. The man Inspector Moon called Williams. The man who could be mixed up in a murder. The man Tim had been talked into keeping an eye on although, the more he thought about it, the more surreal it seemed. Three days had gone by since Inspector Moon turned up on the doorstep; three days he'd spent wondering what to say to Jen the next time he saw her; three days he'd sat twiddling his thumbs.

The sky was getting blacker, the brooding stillness more and more oppressive. A flicker: it couldn't be described as anything more, then seconds later a rumble of thunder far off in the distance.

He wandered slowly back down the lane to the stone pillars where he stared at the warning notice he'd stared at so many times before. There was a stirring in the air, a wind which went as quickly as it came, catching the tops of the trees before dying away again.

Another sound? At first Tim thought he was mistaken but then he heard it again. A car, a long way off but getting closer and close enough for him to realise it was coming up the lane towards him. He looked round for somewhere to hide. Opposite the stone pillars was the overgrown hedge where he'd seen the hooded figure on the day he sat on the ridge. It was thick and full of tangles but he pushed his way into it ignoring the briars and brambles catching against his sleeves. He wasn't a second too soon. A set of headlights appeared, coming over the rise down by the spinney, casting black shadows and forcing him to draw back further into the hedge. A silver Range Rover: he didn't doubt for one minute it was the same Range Rover he'd seen from his spy place up on the ridge. The light was almost gone but, as he craned his neck to get a better view, he saw there were two people sitting inside.

He watched the tail lights of the Range Rover as it rattled across the cattle grid and disappeared around the laurel bushes. What was he expected to do now? He knew the answer because Inspector Moon had made the terms of his deal abundantly clear. He had to brave the threat of being mauled by the mastiff, follow the Range Rover up the driveway, see where it went and at the same time see who Williams was with and what he was up to.

Another flicker of lightning then more thunder, much nearer this time. He stepped across the cattle grid doing his best to put all thoughts of the mastiff out of his head. To his left the clump of laurels while, on his right, a neglected shrubbery with overgrown bushes, some tall and straggly, others squat and rounded. Each step he took his boots made crunching noises on the red shale. Finally, he saw the gables of a house peeping out over the top of an ornamental beech hedge. He paused, counted to three before advancing any further. Yet more thunder and lightning. He bit his lip nervously. Ten yards, twenty yards, one step at a time, until he came round a curve in the drive and there, in front of him, stood an impressive looking mansion with stone mullioned windows and a short flight of steps leading up to a heavily studded front door covered by a portico. The Range Rover was pulled over at the side of the steps, still with its headlights on and its engine idling. He stopped again. The Range Rover was no more than fifty yards from where he stood and a warning voice inside his head was telling him not to get any closer. Over to his right was an ancient looking yew with low overhanging branches almost touching the ground. He cautiously made his way across to it. More lightning, the front of the mansion with its buttresses and heavily-carved stonework transformed fleetingly into something out of a creepy movie. The thunder, when it came, was louder echoing off the hillsides and rolling away across the dale. It was followed by a sudden gust of wind ripping through the trees, picking up small twigs and other pieces of debris. His attention was still firmly fixed on the Range Rover, still with its headlights on, still with its engine running. He stood perfectly still in the dark shadows under the yew tree. Then he remembered the binoculars in his pocket which he fetched out and, just as he did, it started to rain. Big heavy drops hitting the ground with soft plopping noises while the branches of the yew tree acted like a giant umbrella keeping him dry. He raised the binoculars to his eyes but found they were misted up so he couldn't see anything. He put his hand in his pocket and brought out the packet of tissues so he could wipe the lenses. The Range Rover's engine finally stopped and, seconds later the headlights were switched off plunging everything into darkness. More seconds passed. The driver's door opened, a courtesy light came on and a man got out. Tim, meanwhile, had dropped the packet of tissues on the ground and, by the time he managed to find it again, the man had been joined by a woman. Both were now standing under the portico where a lamp hanging from a chain over the door had been switched on.

Swiftly Tim raised the binoculars to his eyes. The two figures had their backs to him: the woman wearing a smart black business suit with a straight skirt and high heels; the man dressed more casually in a tweed jacket and what looked like cavalry twill trousers; the woman checking something in the bag she was carrying; the man sorting through his keys. The man could have been the same man Tim saw from the ridge: heavily-built and hair swept back with a side parting. It was hard to tell.

A flash of lightning again, this one illuminating the sky like a backdrop, picking out the silhouette shapes of the trees followed soon after by another clap of thunder. Tim looked back towards the couple under the portico just in time to see them go through the heavily studded door and close it behind them.

Suddenly and without warning the rain started to come in torrents. What had been a few drops at first turned into a downpour. In the house a light had come on. A large bay window directly in front of where Tim was standing. He raised the binoculars to his eyes again. The man and woman were in a room with panelled walls and a crystal chandelier hanging from a high stuccoed ceiling. He was pouring sherry from a decanter and passing a glass to her. She was standing with her back to the window.

More thunder and lightning: the rain was coming down so heavily now it was penetrating the thick evergreen foliage of the yew tree and starting to drip on Tim's head and shoulders. Still he kept the binoculars trained on the scene in front of him taking in details of the room such as the stone fireplace, books in bookcases and oil paintings on the wall. The woman hadn't moved while the man topped up his glass for the second time. Tim focussed the binoculars on his face: puffy twisted lips parted slightly and eyes as hard as stones. He seemed to be doing something but Tim couldn't see what. Suddenly the woman came to life. She turned her head towards the window so, for the first time, he had a clear view of her face.

He froze and, for a split second, his mind went numb. It was Jen. Not the Jen he knew but Jen wearing make-up and bright red lipstick.

Finally the turmoil of emotions inside him exploded. Still clutching the binoculars, he stepped out of the cover of the yew tree, not caring any longer whether anybody saw him or not. Out in the open with one wild thought after another racing through his head and the wind and rain lashing against him: he stopped short of where the pool of light from the big bay window spilled out onto the ground. Another flash of lightning followed almost immediately by a deafening crash of thunder. His hair was already soaked and plastered to his scalp while Jen had turned round again so she was back facing the man in the tweed jacket. Nothing happened at first then she put her glass down, took a step forward and everything became confusing. One moment the man was standing there, the next he was sinking to his knees and she was pushing past him.

Seconds later Tim heard the sound of the front door opening. He looked across and saw Jen as she came down the short flight of steps. When she reached the bottom she stopped and stood in the rain. It was then that she saw him and the shock was etched on her face. In one hand she had the large pair of scissors he'd last seen on the table in her workroom; in the other she was clutching something.

'I cut his cock off,' she said opening her hand.

A single shaft of lightning split the heavens apart striking somewhere close by accompanied by an enormous clap of thunder which made the ground shake and the air vibrate. The storm was almost on top of them while Jen still stood by the steps with trails of make-up starting to run down her face. He took his coat off and put it round her shoulders then went over to pick her bag up from where she'd dropped it.

A noise of something crashing through the undergrowth: Tim turned round aghast to see the mastiff had appeared from the bushes and was making straight for Jen. She'd seen it too. Pounds of muscle and sinew closing in on her but she didn't move, waiting until it was almost on her, then calmly throwing what she held in her hand to the ground where the mastiff pounced on it greedily.

'Don't run,' said Tim and together they walked away slowly. Back along the driveway passing between the laurels and the neglected shrubbery. Back to where they came to the cattle grid which Jen somehow managed to step across without taking her shoes off. Back up the lane where Tim led the way with thunder and lightning all around them. Back to the hawthorns and where he'd left the car.

Apart from Tim asking her for the keys which were still in the zip-up pocket of his coat, neither of them spoke. They drove back down the lane pausing only briefly by the stone pillars where nothing moved and everything was in darkness.

Safely back at the cottage Tim gave Jen a towel to dry her hair and sat her down in front of the fire. He then changed out of his wet clothes before going through to the kitchen to put on a jug of strong coffee.

'I think I owe you an explanation,' she said as he came and sat down beside her. 'My real name's Jen Rodericks so you're not the only one pretending to be somebody else. The bastard you saw up there is the bastard who raped my little sister and who thought he'd got away with it.' She then told the story of Vicky and what happened to her. Vicky whose life had been ruined. Vicky who only craved love and kindness but who instead was made a victim of wickedness and cruelty. Vicky who now spent her days lost in a world of her own. Unable to share her thoughts with anybody – except the rag doll somebody had given her as a child and who she sat with day after day. Scared even to go out of the house in case he was there waiting for her.

'He thought he was clever when he walked out of court laughing all over his face. I vowed that day I'd see to it he paid for what he'd done.' She reached for her bag which she'd put down by her feet. The scissors were inside and she brought them out studying them in the light of the fire. 'In the end he made it easy,' she said. 'He wanted me to suck him off and he got it out expecting me to go down on my knees at his feet.'

The storm continued to rage outside but, shut out by the curtains and muffled by the cottage's thick stone walls, it seemed like a million miles away. Jen was still talking. 'His name is Leinthall Williams,' she said. 'I thought he might recognise me. I was sitting in court next to Mum and Dad so I grew my hair long and hoped the passage of time would help.'

'You planned all this?'

'Yes. I found out about his business affairs. It took a while to build up a detailed picture of what he did and who he associated with. I followed him when he sold his place in Wrexham.'

'So what happened tonight?'

'His property development company has been inviting quotes for supplying staff to work on a big contract they've got coming up in the Middle East. I posed as someone from a firm of recruitment consultants working on commission.'

'He fell for it?'

'He invited me to his office in Telford but it was his idea we continued discussions over drinks back at his place. He'd made it plain by then what I had to do if I wanted his business.'

'You put yourself in danger?'

'I did it for Vicky's sake.'

'Everything you told me about yourself – your work, your plans for the future – did you make it all up?"

'Did I deceive you? I could say again I did it for Vicky's sake but most of what I told you is true; I want to design and make my own range of fashions. It's all I've ever dreamed of doing.'

'You could go to prison.'

'If I do I'll pick up the pieces when I get out. I'll tell the judge Williams tried to rape me and I fought him off in self-defence.'

'You're not afraid?'

'Why should I be? People like Williams thrive on fear. They pick on the weak and defenceless. They're bullies and the only way is to stand up to them and fight back. At least I made sure Williams won't be ruining the lives of any more innocent little girls.'

When he drove her back to her place the storm had abated. A few flickers of lightning still but they were a long way off while the rain was little more than drizzle. Jen was silent on the short journey, staring out of the side window into the nothingness of the night. When he pulled up outside the bungalow she sat there for a while and made no move to get out. A light was on over the porch shining down on the bare trellises round the front door. The Suzuki van was missing but the black cat was sitting on the doorstep waiting patiently.

'I'll let you into another secret,' she said smiling. 'The grey ghost was me. I made the outfit to keep a watch on Williams from the hedge outside his house where you saw me. I watched you when you came along. You seemed to spend a lot of time in the woods up by his place and I wondered why. I knew he'd made a lot of enemies over the years and I thought you could be one of them.'

'Was that why you befriended me?'

She smiled at him again. 'I'll have to leave you to figure that one out for yourself.'

She leaned over and kissed him lightly on the cheek then she was gone, a slender figure crunching her heels on the gravel and making her way towards the pool of light by the front door. He waited for her to turn round but she didn't. It would be a long time before he saw her again.

EPILOGUE

The body of Leinthall Williams was found two days after the winter thunderstorm which most people agreed was the worst in living memory. The paramedic team who first arrived on the scene quickly determined he died from loss of blood caused by what appeared to be genital mutilation.

Police were brought in who thought at first the wounds were self-inflicted but, as the forensic evidence mounted up, a picture emerged which pointed to foul play. He died with the phone in his hand fuelling speculation he tried to make a '999' call in his final desperate moments. Whether or not it was a contributory factor in his death, the storm had brought the phone lines down and they remained out of order for several days.

News of Williams' fate reached Detective Inspector Charlie Moon shortly afterwards and, later that day, Jo Lyon and he shared a bottle of champagne. It came as no surprise to Moon when he was told that Detective Inspector Millership had been chosen to lead the investigation into Williams' murder and, at the same time, take over the ongoing investigation into the murder of Sean Mattox. After six months both investigations were wound down. No arrests were ever made. Finger prints found on a wine glass in the same room as Williams' body did not match any finger prints held on national criminal records.

Jen Rodericks returned to Wrexham where she acquired the lease on a small industrial unit and went into business designing and manufacturing a range of clothing and fashion accessories. Currently the business employs twenty people and there are plans to expand. Vicky Rodericks works as a sewing machinist in Jen's business, a job she loves and people who know her say how pleased they are to see her out and about again with a smile back on her face.

Less is known of Tim Giffard. He divorced his wife in 2004 and moved first to Sheffield and then to Bristol where he works on fixed term contracts supplied to him by an agency. He sees his son from time to time but his daughter hasn't spoken to him since the divorce. Reports that he still keeps in touch with Jen Rodericks are rumoured but not confirmed.

APPENDIX

Team Penda

The West Midlands Serious Crimes Squad was disbanded in 1989 in the wake of accusations of corruption and wrongdoing on all levels. Among the charges levelled were those of falsification of evidence, big sums handed out to mysterious informers and the ways in which confessions were extracted from suspects held in custody – described by one wag at the time as 'sign here or else'. The impression presented to a shocked public was that of an organisation seriously out of control and past the point of salvation.

Predictably perhaps in the wake of such a debacle came a period for reflection, a hiatus they called it, a time when the culprits were dealt with and the soul searching went on. Then, only as the dust began to settle, did the debate over what was to be done about replacing the Serious Crimes Squad finally get under way.

In country retreats far removed from the hustle and bustle of daily police work, they held meeting after meeting, many of which went on far into the night. On one point they were agreed from the outset: there would be no repeats of what had gone on before. No more homes from home for fiddlers or those who lived by their own rules. Instead a line would be firmly drawn in the sand. Anything in future would be subject to principles of strict accountability and management control and, to this end, they came up with the structure: fragmented and cellular. There would not be one Serious Crimes Squad but several: small ponds where, if anything crawled up out of the slime in the bottom, it would be spotted and dealt with before it did any harm.

So it was that Team Penda was born. Named like its counterparts after the ancient Kings of Mercia within whose long-vanished boundaries the county of the West Midlands lies, it came into being on the wave of what became known in later years as political correctness. It was, in many ways, a natural child of its time.

(from: The Silent Passage)